I'M A CHICKEN, GET ME OUT OF HERE!

Anna Wilson lives in Bradford on Avon with her husband, two children, two cats, one dog and five chickens. She is the author of many young-fiction novels published by Macmillan Children's Books – and while many of them have been about pets, this is the first to feature a talking chicken.

Books by Anna Wilson

The Poodle Problem
The Dotty Dalmatian
The Smug Pug

Puppy Love
Pup Idol
Puppy Power
Puppy Party

Kitten Kaboodle
Kitten Smitten
Kitten Cupid

Monkey Business

www.annawilson.co.uk

I'M A CHICKEN, GET ME OUT OF HERE!

Anna Wilson

ILLUSTRATED BY ANDY ROWLAND

MACMILLAN CHILDREN'S BOOKS

First published 2013 by Macmillan Children's Books
a division of Macmillan Publishers Limited
20 New Wharf Road, London N1 9RR
Basingstoke and Oxford
Associated companies throughout the world
www.panmacmillan.com

ISBN 978-1-4472-3663-4

Text copyright © Anna Wilson 2013
Illustrations copyright © Andy Rowland 2013

The right of Anna Wilson and Andy Rowland to be identified as
the author and illustrator of this work has been asserted by them in
accordance with the Copyright, Designs and Patents Act 1988.

135798642

A CIP catalogue record for this book is available from
the British Library.

Printed and bound by CPI Group (UK) Ltd, Croydon CR0 4YY

For Tom and his amazing Pekin,
Titch, who stayed out all night
and outwitted the fox!

CHAPTER 1

AN EGGS-CITING DELIVERY

'Wilfie, can you hurry up and finish your breakfast?'
Mum called over her shoulder. 'We have to go in
fifteen minutes.'

'Hmm,' said Wilf.

Wilf Peasbody was staring into space and thinking
about the heron he had seen on the way home
yesterday. It had been sitting on the riverbank,
peering patiently into the water, watching and
waiting. It had been so still that Wilf had thought at
first that it might actually be a statue, like the ones
people put by ponds to stop real herons stealing
the goldfish. But this one had immediately proved
it wasn't a statue by taking off, diving dramatically

into the water
and coming out
with a wriggling
silver fish in its beak. Wilf
had held his breath, as he
hadn't wanted the heron to
drop the fish. Then the bird
had made a flicking motion
with its head, flipped the fish
fully into its beak and swallowed
hard: the whole fish had gone down its
throat in one swift movement! The heron's neck
had been fat with its freshly caught meal and had
wriggled slightly as though the fish was struggling to
get out.

Wilf shuddered as he thought about what it
would be like to swallow a whole, live, slithery fish.
Then he looked at the bread roll in front of him and
wondered if he could fit that into his mouth in one
go. It might be a good experiment.

He glanced up to check that Mum was not

watching and shifted his gaze to the left to make sure that his little sister Meena was not about to kick him or pinch him as she usually did, as that would definitely make him choke. Luckily she was busy emptying out the contents of Mum's handbag into the dog's water bowl.

Wilf opened his mouth as wide as it would go, quickly popped the whole roll in and snapped his lips tight shut.

DRIIIING!

'Oh, Wilfie, could you get that?' Mum said. 'I've got my hands full.'

'Yeah, *Wilfie*,' said Meena, her dark blue eyes flashing as she dropped Mum's expensive lipstick into the water with a satisfying splash. 'You go. Unless you've got your MOUTH full . . .'

Wilf narrowed his eyes at his sister and wished he could tell Mum what Meena was doing, but his cheeks were bulging with bread. He pushed his chair back and ran to the door before Mum could see his face.

3

DRIIIIING! The bell rang more insistently, and Wilf hurled himself at the door, opening it just in time to see a van drive away at breakneck speed, screeching round the corner, doing one of those handbrake turns that gangsters do in car chases on the telly.

'Eh?' he said. Except he couldn't actually say anything, as his cheeks were still bunged full with bread roll, which was now getting a bit mushy and

4

quite difficult to handle. (Herons must need that extra-long neck to be able to deal with this sort of thing, he realized, a bit too late.) He looked down and saw a medium-sized cardboard box on the doorstep with an address label on it that was clearly marked 'Mrs B. Peasbody, 12 Clematis Drive'.

Ringo the dog appeared by his side, looking up at him expectantly just as he was wondering what he was going to do  with the breakfast that he could not swallow.

Wilf checked that Mum had not followed him to the door, then he scooped the soggy mush out of his mouth and gave it to Ringo, who gobbled it up gratefully.

'Thanks, Ringo,' he said, turning his attention to the box.

Ringo licked his chops as if to say, 'The pleasure's all mine.'

Wilf gazed at the box and wondered exactly what sort of online order his mother had placed this time.

'I hope it's not something that *we* have to get involved with,' he said with feeling. 'Do you remember that time she got a juicer and she made us drink spinach juice for breakfast to make sure we got enough Vitamin C and iron?'

Ringo flattened his ears, put his tail between his legs and whimpered. Even *he* had drawn the line at puréed spinach first thing in the morning.

Or any other time, come to that.

'Wilf?' his mother called from the kitchen. 'Who was that at the door? Have you finished your breakfast yet? And have you cleaned your teeth? And . . .'

'What's in the box?' Meena had crept up behind him and snatched the parcel from under his nose. She immediately began shaking it.

Ringo saw that a game was about to begin and he was not going to be left out, so he started jumping up and barking his excited, happy bark.

'Rrrooooooowww!' he yelped.

'Down, boy,' Wilf commanded. Then he lunged at his sister. 'Gimme that. I'm the one who answered the door.'

'And *I'm* the one who picked up the box,' Meena retaliated.

'Mine.'

'Mine.'

'Raooowfff!' barked Ringo.

Mum came running. 'What on earth is this racket about? And who has been feeding Ringo bread again? You know it disagrees with him.' She inspected the nasty mess that Ringo, in his excitement, had deposited on the hall carpet.

Mum stepped over the sticky nastiness, stood between her squabbling children and lifted the box neatly from their grasping hands. 'Wilf, go and get some cloths and some disinfectant. Meena, go back

to the kitchen and finish your breakfast. Ringo –
basket!'

Ringo immediately stopped barking and slunk
away, tail between his legs.

'Hssssss,' said Ned the cat, who was watching the
scene from a safe distance.

Ringo shot Ned a sorrowful look and trudged
slowly to his basket in the kitchen.

'OK, Mum,' said Wilf, 'but open the parcel now!'

'Yes, Mummy. Please open it,' said Meena. She
had put on her most wide-eyed and innocent look,
which she always reserved for grown-ups. That,
together with her golden locks and dark blue eyes,
seemed to make all adults convinced that she was an
angel (that's how stupid grown-ups can be).

'Come on, sweetie,' Mum said to her little
daughter, her expression melting. 'Let's take it
into the kitchen. You can open it while Wilf helps
me clear the table. I have no idea what it can be,'
she added, frowning. 'I haven't ordered anything
recently.'

8

Wilf rolled his eyes. His mother could never remember when she had ordered something or *what* she had ordered. He only hoped it was not something that would make his life a misery.

CHAPTER 2

HOW CLUCKY IS THAT?

Meena waited until Mum had turned her back to walk towards the kitchen, then stuck her tongue out, pinched Wilf and ran off before he could pinch her back.

'Hey—!' began Wilf, but he was interrupted.

By the box.

'Beeuuuuuurrrckk!' said the box.

'Wilf,' said Mum, wheeling round. 'There's no need to be rude.'

'But I didn't say anything,' Wilf protested.

'Buuuuueeeeeeeuuuurrccck!' said the box again. This time it was really loud.

Mum jumped. Wilf dropped the box, and Meena

10

rushed to open it. Wilf rushed too and banged his head against Meena's. Then he stepped back and trod in Ringo's bread-sick, and then Ringo came running back again and began jumping and barking even more than before.

'STOP!' Mum screamed.

Everybody stopped in the middle of what they were doing: Ringo stopped in mid-air, which meant he came crashing down to earth rather suddenly and hurt his bottom. He whined and sloped back off to his basket again without being told.

The box was rocking from side to side now and letting out weird chirruping noises.

'Oh dear,' said Mum. 'I'm not sure I like the sound of this.'

'I do!' said Wilf, who thought he might have guessed what it was already.

'I do,' mimicked Meena, but softly so that Mum did not catch her doing it.

Mum was, in fact, already concentrating on gently lifting the box on to the kitchen table. She then went to fetch a pair of scissors and carefully slit the tape on the top, pulled the flaps apart and peered cautiously in.

'OH!' she cried, taking a step back. 'OH, MY GOODNESS.'

'Beeurrrucck!' said the box. And a small, pale grey head appeared through the open flaps and fixed Wilf with a beady-eyed look, which plainly said, 'How on earth did I get here?'

'How on earth did that – that *thing* get here?' Mum said.

The chicken – for that is what it was – squawked in a most offended tone, leaving the box with a flutter of her wings to land on the kitchen table.

'I don't think she likes being called a "thing",' said Wilf. He had spotted an envelope in the box and was now carefully reading the contents. 'I think she's a rather special kind of hen, actually,' he added.

'Ooooh, "rather special",' whispered Meena, jabbing her brother in the ribs.

'OOooW!' shouted Wilf.

'Give me that,' Mum said, snatching the letter. 'And stop fighting with your sister, Wilf.'

'But—!'

'Ah, this will be the returns label,' Mum said with relief.

'Is that the piece of paper you always use to stick on the parcels you send back, Mummy?' asked Meena, who was wearing her sweetness-and-light expression again.

'Yes, dear,' said Mum. 'We can put the hen back in the box now and . . .'

Mum tailed off. Her face had gone very pale and she was shaking her head and muttering, 'No, no, this can't be right.'

'What's the matter, Mummy?' asked Meena.

'It's not a returns label,' said Mum.

'No, but there is an Instructions for Care letter instead,' said Wilf importantly. He stood on tiptoes to see the letter Mum was still holding shakily and read out loud what it said.

EXCELLENT PETS

Congratulations on becoming the proud owner of a Lavender Pekin bantam hen.

The first Pekins are said to have been given as a gift to Queen Victoria from a Chinese emperor.

Pekins are very gentle and they make excellent pets for children. They need little space and they love company.

'They sound great!' Wilf added, beaming with delight. '*Excellent* pets!' he repeated with emphasis. 'How lucky is that?'

'Don't you mean, "How *clucky*"?' Meena sniggered.

'That's as may be,' said Mum. 'But you know my view on pets, Wilfred.'

Sadly, Wilf did know Mum's views on pets, only too well. And it did not coincide with *his* view on pets, which was simply that pets were what made life interesting. He was about to say as much, but Mum was already shaking her head.

'We have enough animals to look after as it is,' she said.

'But, Mu-um!' Wilf began.

'Listen, dear, it's not that I don't like the pets we have. It's just that we cannot possibly have any more. We have talked about this before . . .' She tailed off and peered suspiciously at her son. 'Did YOU order this hen over the internet?'

'No, I did not!' Wilf protested. He was very indignant that Mum should suggest such a thing.

If Mum really hadn't done it in one of her absent-minded online shopping splurges, it was much more likely to have been Meena than him. She was always getting up to no good. (Like now, for instance, she was taking advantage of the confusion to climb on to the kitchen work surface and post grapes out of the kitchen window one at a time on to the bird table.)

'Beeeuuuurrck?' said the hen. She had fluffed up her feathers, Wilf noticed, and seemed to be trying to make herself look as appealing as possible. It was certainly working, as far as Wilf was concerned.

'Hmmm,' said Mum. 'I wouldn't be surprised if your grandmother was behind this . . .'

Wilf's grandma was an animal-lover, just as Wilf was. In fact, she was the only grown-up person he knew who seemed genuinely to like animals more than people.

'If Grandma ordered the hen, it would be rude to send it back without asking her first, wouldn't it?' said Wilf.

Mum opened her mouth to say she thought it

was rather rude to buy such a stupid thing without asking *her* first when there was a loud hissing noise, a blur of black fur and a screech from the Pekin.

Ned the cat had somehow found his way on to the table without anyone noticing, which only goes to show how distracted everyone was by the hen, as Ned was so fat he was not usually so easily missed. He was making his presence felt now, however, by circling the hen with a look of evil intent written all over his face.

'NO!' shouted Wilf.

'Miaaaooooow!' shrieked Ned.

'Cluuuuuckk-uck-ccccukk!' cried the hen, opening her wings wide and flying into the cat's face.

'Wuffff! Wuff!' shouted Ringo, his paws on the table.

'How did the cat get up there? Get him off!' exclaimed Mum.

Wilf dived on to Ned and held him, while Mum flapped her arms and ran round in circles, trying to get Ringo out of the room. (Looking rather like a chicken herself, Wilf thought.) As Wilf wrestled with Ned, he caught a glimpse of Meena slinking away with a devious look on her face.

'Hey! Meena—' Wilf began. In that split second he knew that his sister had been solely responsible for the chaotic scene (although, if asked, he would not have been able to explain exactly how she had achieved it).

But Wilf's little sister had already made good her escape, and now Mum was glaring at him. He hurriedly removed the scratching, spitting Ned, who was not at all amused at having his Hen Hunt interrupted. Wilf carried him out to the garden, stroking him and making soothing cooing noises all the while to calm him down.

'What about the chicken, Wilfred?' Mum had worked herself up into a frenzy and was shouting at him through the French windows. Her face had gone a curious shade of raspberry. 'You can't leave *that* on the table too! And how did all my make-up and money get into Ringo's bowl? And why have you eaten all the grapes? I only bought them yesterday and . . .'

Wilf turned his back on Mum and dropped Ned on to the patio. But Ringo had chosen that moment to race out of the house, so that Ned landed on him instead of the flagstones. Ringo immediately ran back into the house, round and round in circles, to show off his fat and furry headgear. Although he did stop pretty sharpish once Ned decided to dig his claws in.

'Yoooowlll!'

'Miaaaaooooow!'

'BeeeurrrRRRRRCKKKK!' The little hen had clearly had enough of her new home already and was flying around the room in a blind panic, bashing her head against the ceiling and smacking against the door and windows in a desperate attempt to escape. She seemed not to have noticed the open French windows, which Wilf thought was rather stupid of her.

'Get the dog out! Get the cat out!' Mum cried, coming back inside. 'Ooooh! I thought chickens

couldn't fly! This is a disaster!'

'Of course chickens can fly,' said Wilf disdainfully.
'They have wings, don't they?'

Glaring at Wilf by way of reply, Mum grabbed
Ringo as he went whizzing past, with Ned still
clinging to him, and shooed them both out of the
house. Wilf managed to catch the hen and held on
to her, whispering to her to calm her down. Mum
slammed the French windows shut and peace was
restored.

'Right,' Mum panted. 'You had better put that hen
straight back in the box. You are going to be late for
school and I am going to be late for work. And where
is Meena? Oh dear, she was probably frightened by
all the kerfuffle.'

'But we can't leave the hen shut in a box all day!'
Wilf protested. 'She'll starve!'

'FINE!' Mum shouted. 'Give her some water and
something to eat. But she will have to stay in the box
until tea. We haven't got time for this!'

'I'll look after you,' Wilf told the little Pekin. He

put a small pot of cornflakes into the box along with some water. 'Don't you worry. Grandma is coming to visit. She will help me to convince Mum that you can stay.'

The Pekin put her head on one side and stared at him coolly. Wilf had a sinking feeling that, after the way the hen had been welcomed, staying at the Peasbodys' was not proving to be a very attractive idea at all. 🐔

CHAPTER 3

GETTING IN A FLAP

At last the house was quiet. Ringo had been let back in, but was now snoozing in his basket, evidently exhausted by the morning's drama; Ned was nowhere to be seen. When the Peasbodys had finally left the house for school and work, the Pekin fluffed her feathers and scratched mournfully at the floor of the cardboard box. This had not been part of her plan.

'When I left the chicken run, I thought I would be going to a better life. I thought I would be exploring the world, seeing the sights, stretching my wings!' she twittered sadly. 'I did not bank on such an unfriendly reception.'

'Oh, do stop moaning,' said a low voice from outside the box. 'At least you are safe in there.'

The Pekin jumped and hit her head for the second time that morning. 'Who's that?'

'It's me, the one you had a go at just now,' said the voice.

'Me? Had a go at? What?' squawked the hen.

There was the sound of violent scratching on the outside of the box. The terrified chicken backed herself into a corner. She looked up at where the noise was coming from and saw that something was opening the top of the box. A moment later, a black face appeared in the opening.

'Get away from me!' shrieked the hen. 'I'm warning you! I'll scratch your eyes out!'

'Yes, yes, I'm sure you will,' said Ned carelessly. He thrust one sharpened claw through the opening and bared his teeth. 'But, just so you know, I can give every bit as good as I get in a fight. And I am certainly not frightened of you.'

'Oh,' said the hen, lifting her head in a haughty

24

manner. 'Well, that's just as well, because I am not frightened of you either.'

Ned gave a snorty purr. 'Which is why you got in such a flap just now, I suppose?' he sneered.

The hen flew up at him, her wings wide. 'Now listen to me, you – you – what exactly *are* you, anyway?' she asked, hovering at the top of the box.

'I, my feathered friend, am a cat,' said Ned smoothly.

'A cat? A CAT?' the Pekin screeched. She flew at Ned, her feet out in front of her like daggers. 'I've heard all about you cats! You are one of those whatchamacallits – an Arch-Enemy. Not to be trusted!'

'Oh, for goodness sake. Keep your feathers on, will you? You are in no danger from me – I am very well fed by the family – and even if I was looking for something to eat it would have to be something a lot tastier than you. I prefer a rather more *gourmet* diet, if you know what I mean.' He shot the hen a very disparaging look. 'All those feathers of

25

yours – terribly bad for the digestion. No, no: my meals always come pre-prepared with only the best ingredients.'

'Beeuuurrck!' protested the Pekin. 'You, sir, are very distasteful, not to say rude!'

Ned gave one paw a thoughtful lick. 'I am also the best chance you will have of surviving this madhouse, so do stop chirruping at me and listen.'

The hen hopped back down on to the floor of the box. She needed a moment to think things through. It was true that Ned was a very large cat who certainly did not look in need of more food, but how did she know he was not lying when he said he was not interested in eating her? Maybe he was planning to capture her now and eat her later?

'All right then,' she said slyly, 'I'll listen to you if you let me out. It's awfully hard to hear what you're saying from in here.'

The cat raised his eyebrows. 'If you think I'm falling for that . . .' he said. 'Honestly, we felines invented the word "crafty". I know what you'll do if I open the box. You'll be out of here and away, and I will get the blame when the family comes home and finds an empty box and a few scattered feathers. Oh no, you are staying right where you are.'

The hen sighed noisily. 'I am *not*,' she said sulkily. 'That is the last thing I am doing. I am going to get out of this box, out of this house and out into the big wide world as soon as I can. Just you watch me.'

Ned's eyes widened. 'I would simply *love* to watch you,' he said in a disbelieving tone. 'I would love to see how you think you are going to get past the Terror, for a start.'

'What are you talking about now?' snapped the hen.

'All I can say is that you had better start scrabbling about for that "returns label" Mrs Peasbody was talking about,' hissed Ned, 'because unless you get down from your high horse and let me help you that's the only way you are going to be getting out of some very hot water.'

CHAPTER 4

CLAWS-TROPHOBIA

Later that day, Mum, Wilf and Grandma were sitting around the table discussing what should happen to the Pekin. Or 'Titch', as Wilf had already named her. Wilf had got her out of the box as soon as he had come home from school (*much* against Mum's will) and had her on his lap while they discussed her future.

'I am going to Google all the farms and chicken breeders in the area,' said Mum. 'One of them is sure to take her off our hands if I can't find out where she came from.'

'Talking of Google, have you checked your internet history, dear?' asked Grandma, using her careful and patient voice.

'Yes, thank you,' Mum answered crisply. 'I have checked and I have definitely not been ordering Pekin hens in my sleep.'

'Maybe you thought you were requesting *Peking duck* when you did your last online supermarket order,' Grandma smirked. 'It wouldn't be the first time you had made a mistake on the internet.'

It cannot be emphasized enough: Wilf's mother really did do a *lot* of internet shopping. And thankfully it was not just horrible things like juicers that she ordered. Sometimes she ordered a year's supply of Wilf's favourite cereal because it was on special offer. Sometimes she ordered rolls of carpet, not because the Peasbody family needed rolls of carpet, but because there was a deal on carpets that was 'too good to pass by'. And Grandma was right: she had made mistakes in the past. There was the time she had taken delivery of 500 cucumbers when she had wanted only five. Mum had made them eat cucumber with everything. She had even made a cucumber cake. Wilf had never wanted to see a cucumber again after that episode.

'Anyway,' said Wilf, 'I am calling her Titch and she is staying.' He raised his voice before the conversation could go off track and he lost his chance altogether. He was patting the hen while holding on to her firmly to prove his point.

He had to hold on to her firmly as she had already tried more than once to free herself from his grasp.

'Titch? *Weird* name,' Meena said softly so that only Wilf could hear. 'Sounds like "itch". Maybe it's got fleas? Are you feeling *itchy*, Wilfie?' she said, tipping some biscuit crumbs down the back of his neck.

Wilf squirmed and tried to scratch himself on the chair back without using his hands to avoid letting go of the hen.

'Don't you have anything better to do?' asked Wilf angrily. 'Anyway, she's a she, not an it.'

'How do *you* know?' Meena said.

Wilf looked fondly at the little bird. 'She's obviously a she,' Wilf said. 'And anyway, she hasn't said "cock-a-doodle-doo" and it said she was a hen on the "Instructions for Care" letter, not a cockerel.'

'She's very cute,' Grandma said, following Wilf's gaze. 'And ever so warm and cuddly. And it does say in that letter that she will make an excellent pet.'

She winked at Wilf, who grinned gratefully in response.

'You are most definitely *not* helping,' Mum grumbled.

'Titch,' said Meena. 'Itchy, scratchy Titchy . . .' She made her eyes go big and did silly kissing noises.

'Stop doing that,' Wilf said. 'She's not a baby. Or a cat.'

As if on cue, Ned appeared.

'How does that cat do it?' Mum said.

He had found his way into the house, in spite of the fact that Mum had shut all the doors and checked all exits and entrances.

He was stalking around Wilf's legs and weaving in and out of the chair legs too, giving off a low, warning growl every so often, and curling and swishing his tail as though trying to lasso the bird and pull her off Wilf's lap. He was also licking his lips.

Wilf said nervously, 'I think if we can't keep Ned away we should take Titch somewhere safe.'

33

'Exactly, Wilf,' said Mum. 'And that "somewhere safe", as you put it, is the place she came from. In other words, we are sending her back.'

Wilf clutched Titch firmly to him. 'I've told you already – I did *not* order her!' he said. 'Grandma's right. It was probably you, Mum. You are the one who is always on the computer ordering things.'

'Wilfred Peasbody!' Mum said through gritted teeth. 'For the last time—'

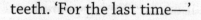

'She's just pooed,' announced Meena, beaming. She pointed to her shoes, which were directly underneath the little hen.

Ringo was by now well-practised in his role, and immediately Hoovered up the mess and sat back licking his chops in a bemused fashion like a wine taster, as though trying to work out what vintage of chicken poo he had been lucky enough to try.

'Disgusting!' cried Mum. 'Oh, I can't bear it. Ringo eats too many unspeakable things as it is. That's it!

Put her back in the box she arrived in. I'll fetch some Sellotape and then you can take her to the post office,' she said to Grandma.

'Gran'maaaa!' Wilf howled as Mum tried to take the hen off him. 'Tell her you can't.'

'I can't. She might get *claws*-trophobia – get it? Claws? Claustrophobia? Haha!' Grandma chuckled at her own joke. Mum rolled her eyes and was about to protest, so Grandma said hastily, 'Anyway, I definitely can't send her back if you don't have a returns label. And the post office is closed now,' she added.

'Beuurccckkk!' Titch said indignantly. She was clearly not happy.

Grandma listened to the clucking and fussing coming from the small chicken and chuckled. 'She certainly doesn't seem to like the idea of being put back inside that box any more than you do, Wilf,' she said. 'Why don't you put her in with Brian? That will at least mean she is out of the house. And safe from Ned,' she added, eyeing the prowling feline. 'The information does say that Pekins like company, after all. And that they don't need much space.'

Mum huffed and puffed. 'We-ell, I don't know . . .'

'Think about the eggs,' continued Grandma. 'Oh, there's nothing better than a fresh egg for breakfast.'

Meena laughed. 'They'll be TITCHY eggs!'

'Exactly,' said Mum.

'Oh, good one!' Grandma giggled. '*Eggs*-actly. Get it?'

'Beuuuurrrcckkkk!' protested Titch.

'You're all upsetting her,' said Wilf.

'I'm not surprised,' said Mum. 'Your grandmother's jokes upset *me* on a regular basis.'

Grandma made a big show of looking hurt, which made Wilf giggle too. Then he said, 'I'm going to do what Grandma says and put her in with Brian until we can build a proper chicken run.'

'A what?' cried Mum.

'I think Wilfie's right, actually, Mummy,' Meena simpered. She sidled up to Mum and hugged her leg. 'The chickie is really, really cute. And titchy eggs

36

would be just the right size for me, wouldn't they, Mummy?'

Wilf was puzzled. It was not normal for his sister to be on his side about anything. What was she up to?

But then, he reasoned, why should he care what she was up to, if her powers of persuasion meant that Mum might change her mind? And, by the look on her face, it seemed she might be about to do just that. Wilf held his breath and waited . . .

Mum made an exasperated noise. 'Dooohhh!' Then she swung Meena up on to her hip and kissed her on the head. 'I suppose you're right, baby,' she cooed. 'What harm could it possibly do to have another pet around the place? Especially one that lays delicious eggs!'

CHAPTER 5

OUT OF CLUCK

So Titch did escape the 'madhouse'. But if she thought she was escaping to freedom she was to be sorely disappointed. Wilf and Grandma took her out into the garden where she had a brief glimpse of green grass and shady trees and bright blue sky. But she was immediately set down in another box. Admittedly it was less dark than the one in which she had arrived at the Peasbodys': this had wire mesh across one side, which let in light. But it was still a box.

'A prison, more like,' chirruped poor Titch.

She looked about her new home. Her feathers were distinctly ruffled and she felt sure her beak was out of joint.

'This is preposterous,' she said, scratching and fussing. 'How dare the boy treat me in this way? I should not be here. I am a CHICKEN for heaven's sake. And if anyone out there is listening, will you please GET ME OUT OF HERE?'

Sadly, no one did seem to be listening.

Titch sat down and tucked her head under her wing while she thought for a moment. Then, when no great brainwave sprang to mind, she popped her head back out and looked around.

'I may as well get my bearings and make myself comfortable,' she said glumly.

She had noticed that there was lots of lovely bedding, which was a welcome sight after the discomfort of the cardboard box. The very idea of snuggling into it made her feel like taking a nap right away. And someone had helpfully made it into little mounds that were just the right size for nest-building. She considered hunkering down there and then, but caught a whiff of a particularly tempting aroma coming from a small white pot in the far

39

corner of the coop. The cereal that Wilf had fed her earlier had not made much of an impact on the hungry hen, so she was thrilled to find more food had been put out for her.

'Hmmm!' she cooed as she dipped her beak into the pot. 'Corn *and* cornflakes . . . and seeds! And – oh! I wonder what these yummy squashed green things are?' She had a tentative nibble. 'No idea, but they are *delicious*. That boy evidently knows how to care for a hen after all. I should not have been so hasty to judge him. Hmm, I must remember to lay him a double-yolker as a special treat. But first things first!'

She pecked and swallowed and chirruped with delight, making quick work of the pot of food.

'I could take the remains of this meal over to one of the nesting piles,' she said to herself. 'It would be lovely to have a little snooze followed by a late morning breakfast in bed. I feel quite exhausted after all those goings-on in the house.'

She latched on to the side of the pot and dragged

it along the ground. Then, setting the pot down right next to the pile of bedding, she bustled and scratched about until she had made a wonderfully cosy little indentation in the fluffy sawdust mound.

'Aaah!' she sighed. She nestled down, closed her eyes, fluffed her feathers and was soon fast asleep, all ideas of egg-laying immediately forgotten.

*

As Titch slept, she dreamed of rolling green hills and of a small yet friendly community of like-minded feathery friends. She felt the warmth of the sun on her shiny red comb and she purred with happiness, her eyes half closed against the light.

'I shall stay out here forever,' she said to herself. 'I shall be safe and warm and free and – OH! BEURRRRCKKKK! STOP IT!'

Titch woke up with start to find herself face to face with a blur of nasty spiky little claws and pointy teeth.

'A rat?' she squealed. Titch knew all about rats. Rats were worse than cats. Rats were the Archest of Arch-Enemies. Rats gave nasty bites and swiped at you with their claws. They were bullies. Rats stole food. And freshly laid eggs. And . . .

'GERROFFF ME!' she squawked as the rat had another go at her. She scrabbled out of her nest and opened her wings to make herself look huge, scary and imposing. Then she kicked her feet out high in the face of the intruder and with much cawing and furious screeching she set off a rumpus fit to wake the sleepiest of hibernating creatures.

'Ow! Ouch! YOU get off ME!' squeaked the stranger. He backed away and squashed himself against the far wall. 'You're the one who's broken in and stolen my food. I was only protecting what is mine by rights.'

But Titch was not interested in what her attacker had to say, rights or no rights. She was now airborne, feathers flying, wings kicking up bedding and food, her head hitting the ceiling in her panicked attempt to escape. 'Let me out! I want to get out!' she screamed.

'AND I WANT YOU OUT TOO! THIS IS MY HOUSE!' the stranger shouted, rearing up on his funny little stumpy legs.

At this, Titch finally came down to earth with a bump. '*Your* house?' she exclaimed. Now that she inspected the creature closely, she saw that he was not the terrifying rat that she had assumed him to

be. For a start, he did not appear to have a long and horrible tail. And his face was rounder and decidedly more appealing than that of a rat (although it was furry, and it had to be said that Titch was not keen on furry faces, as a rule). His colouring was an interesting combination of orangey-brown, black and white, and his fur seemed to swirl over his body in spirally shapes.

'What on earth *are* you?' Titch asked. She opened her wings wide again to emphasize that she would not stand for any more nonsense. Cute face or not, he had sharp claws, and you had to be prepared.

The creature squeaked and backed further into a corner. 'I could ask you the exact same thing,' he said. 'And, seeing as this is MY house and you have broken in and stolen MY food and ruined MY bedding, I think that is exactly what I will ask: what on earth are you? And what do you think you are doing here?'

Titch let out a warble of disgust. 'Bueeeerrrrck!' she tutted. 'I am a Lavender Pekin, a rare and beautiful hen. And this is my new home.'

'It most certainly is not,' shrieked the creature. 'It is *my* home. I am a tortoiseshell Abyssinian guinea pig, of the species *Cavia porcellus* (according to that know-it-all cat). And we pigs are very particular indeed about hygiene and tidiness. Something I can see we do *not* share with *your* species.' He twitched his nose as he surveyed the mess Titch had made. 'I hope you've had your vaccinations,' he muttered. Then, 'And what is your name, may I ask?'

Titch gave a little harrumphing noise and then said, 'I had a perfectly good name before I ended up being renamed by those humans indoors. I was called Mei Li, which means "beautiful". Those idiots have called me Titch.'

The guinea pig wrinkled his nose. 'Think yourself lucky. My real name is José-Maria Manuel de Torres,

45

but those "idiots", as you call them, have named me Brian.'

Titch sniggered. 'You don't sound very Abyssinian,' she said, 'especially with a name like Brian.'

The guinea pig nibbled one paw in an embarrassed fashion. 'Yes, well. *You* don't sound Chinese, do you? And as I say, Brian is what THEY call me – not my choice. I'm from Peru, anyway, not Abyssinia—'

'But you said—'

'Oh, what's the point in explaining? I've been living here so long, it doesn't matter where I'm from originally,' the guinea pig sniffed. 'At least the family looks after me. I mean, they give me delicious food and lots of comfy bedding and the boy comes in once a week to refresh my environment so, frankly, who am I to complain? Except—' He stopped abruptly as though he was about to say something else but had changed his mind.

Titch put her head on one side and waited. 'Except what?' she said finally.

 46

Brian stared back at her and then said, 'You say you have been renamed by the family?'

Titch nodded.

The guinea pig looked thoughtful. 'Hmm. I suppose I'll have to get used to you then,' he said. 'Just as I have had to get used to that bossy feline and that frankly insane excuse for a dog. If they've renamed you, you'll be staying. But NOT here – not if I have anything to do with it,' he said darkly.

Titch bristled. 'I don't see that you *can* have anything to do with it. The boy brought me out here. But don't worry, I have no desire to stay. I fully intend to get out of here as soon as I can. I am an adventurous hen, and I do not intend to sit around waiting for life to happen to me,' she said, raising her voice in an indignant cluck. 'In any case, it is not natural for a hen to share living arrangements with a tail-less rat.'

'A – a *what*?' Brian squealed. 'I bear no relation whatsoever to those filthy creatures, and I will absolutely *not* be insulted in my own residence!

47

I hate to break it to you, but if you have been put in here it is very unlikely that you will be able to get out until one of the family comes to liberate you. They decide everything when it comes to entering or leaving this place. Why, only this morning I was enjoying myself doing a spot of spring cleaning when the Terror came along and lifted me out.' He gave a little shudder. 'The next thing I knew I had been transferred to someone else's pocket! I might never have seen my lovely home again if I had not decided to sink my teeth into the hand that appeared. I was picked up and flung on to the grass and have only just been returned home.'

'That sounds awful!' Titch exclaimed. The story momentarily distracted her from thinking of her own plight. 'Whose pocket had you been put into?'

'Apparently it was the milkman's. I heard the mother say to him that it was his own fault if he got bitten as he shouldn't have been trying to steal the family's pets! The Terror never gets caught playing her nasty tricks.'

 48

Titch felt a flutter of panic. 'Why don't you run away from this "Terror"?'

Brian gave a high-pitched laugh. 'It's impossible! Unless you know a way of opening a door that is locked from the outside?' He gestured to a wire-meshed panel.

'You mean you can't come and go as you please?' asked Titch.

'See for yourself,' said Brian.

The little hen hopped over to the door and tilted her head so that she could squint at the fastening. There appeared to be a bolt keeping the hutch securely closed.

Brian was right: they were locked in.

CHAPTER 6

A CAT MAY LOOK AT A BOY

Wilf awoke the next morning worrying about Titch.
What if Mum changed her mind about letting him
keep the hen and found a new home for her while he
was at school?

'I could hide her in my bedroom,' he said to
himself as he stretched and got out of bed. 'No,
that wouldn't work,' he sighed, and fumbled in
his cupboard for his uniform. 'She would poo
over all my clothes and toys and things.' He
pulled on a crumpled pair of trousers and put on
yesterday's socks before sitting down again, deep
in thought. 'And even if I could find a special place
in my room that would be a good home for a hen,

50

Meena would be sure to tell Mum.'

Ned padded in softly and began a low, rumbling purr at the sight of Wilf sitting half dressed on the floor. Not for the first time, Wilf found himself envying Ned. The cat did not have to have baths or get dressed or clean his teeth or eat vegetables. Life would be so much better as a cat, Wilf thought. He got on to all fours to approach his pet.

'Hello, Ned,' he said, sniffing gently at the cat and bumping noses with him. 'What do you think? Should I hide Titch?'

'Miaaaaoow,' said Ned. He rubbed his head

against Wilf's cheek affectionately.

'Exactly,' said Wilf. 'What would be the point in having a pet that you had to hide all the time?'

Ned sat down abruptly and glared at Wilf. 'Raaoow!' he declared.

'Well, I'm glad you agree,' said Wilf. He knelt up, his head on one side, and considered his cat carefully.

Wilf often spoke to his pets. Not that they spoke back to him in human language of course. But still, Wilf found that his pets were by far the most intelligent members of the Peasbody family. In fact, Wilf was of the opinion that ALL animals were superior to humans. Apart from Grandma. She was in the same category as the pets. She was almost as cool as a cat, but she was friendlier. And her jokes were funnier. Cats could not tell jokes. At least, not as far as Wilf knew.

'Listen, Ned,' Wilf went on. 'You have got to stop frightening Titch. We can't have any more of you pouncing on her like you did indoors.'

'Miaoooow!' The cat turned his head away from Wilf as though he was offended by the boy's comment. Then he made to lift his back leg and give himself a wash as though he had better things to do than listen to Wilf. Sadly the effect was spoilt by Ned losing his balance and falling over.

Wilf chuckled. 'You're getting too fat, Ned!' he said. 'We'll have to stop feeding you that special cat food and put you on dry biscuits.'

Ned flicked his ears and waved his tail irritably.

Wilf peered at Ned with interest. 'I wonder if you *can* understand me?' he mused. Then, 'Bet you can't,' he said sadly. 'Oh, I *wish* I could speak animal languages. Maybe I am just not trying hard enough. Maybe I should sit very, very still and concentrate very, very hard and then maybe I would finally hear what you are saying.'

At this Ned let out a prolonged hiss, baring his teeth. Then he pranced haughtily out of the room. If Wilf had had to take a guess at what *that* meant, he would have said that Ned was telling him he did not have a hope in heaven of understanding a single word.

'Wilfred!' His mother was shouting up the stairs at him. 'Will you please get a move on? Grandma will be ready to take you to school in ten minutes and she doesn't want to be late.'

Wilfred knew this was not true. Grandma did not care about being late; it was Mum who cared about these things. Grandma liked to say, 'I've got all the time in the world, my dear,' which could not have been, strictly speaking, true, as she was getting very old, so surely she had *less* time than other people?

However, this morning, Wilf was more grateful than usual for the fact that Grandma was taking him to school. He had some very important things to talk to her about, and, as it was a Friday, Meena would not be in the car with them. She had only just started in the infant class and they did not have Friday school until after Christmas, so she was staying at home with Mum, who did not work on Fridays. Wilf was sometimes jealous of this, but it did mean he got Grandma to himself, which kind of made up for it.

Wilf hopped into the kitchen.

'Why are you hopping?' Mum asked, frowning.

'I left one of my shoes down here last night,' Wilf said, looking about him. 'Have you seen it?'

'No!' Mum snapped. 'And I haven't got time to start searching high and low for it now. Oh, Wilf . . .'

Wilf shifted his gaze to his sister, who was busy feeding her breakfast to Ringo while Mum wasn't looking. This would have been all right if her breakfast was something sensible, such as toast, for example. But it wasn't. It was marshmallows, which she had found in the cupboard and had then decided had gone 'a bit gross and crispy around the edges', so she had not wanted to eat them after all.

'Meena, have you seen Wilfred's shoe?' Mum asked in exasperation.

Meena sat up abruptly, dropping the rest of the packet of marshmallows at Ringo's feet. Her face was slightly pink, but her angelic expression had returned, just in time. 'No, Mummy. Sorry, Mummy.'

Wilf hopped right around the kitchen table twice, partly looking for his shoe, but mainly to see if he could manage twice round without falling over. Birds quite often stood on one leg for ages, he thought. He had seen ducks do it by the pond in the park. How did they manage? he wondered as his leg began to feel a bit sore. He went round the table one last time for luck. Only it wasn't lucky, as Meena stuck out her foot and tripped him up.

He was just about to tell Mum what Meena had done when he saw what was sitting right underneath one of her feet, as though it had just been kicked off.

He dived underneath the table and resurfaced with his lost shoe in one hand and waved it in the air. 'Meena was wearing it!' he yelled triumphantly.

'I was not!' Meena protested. 'Ringo took it.'

Mum sighed and looked at her watch. 'I don't really care who took it, just put it on, Wilf.'

Wilf obediently crammed his foot into the shoe and then howled in disgust. He pulled it hastily off again and tipped it upside down. A cascade of marshmallow-coloured lumpy, liquidy yuck came pouring out.

Mum's face went purple. 'I am losing the will to live,' she hissed.

'I wish Wilfie would do that,' whispered Meena.

Grandma came down to breakfast just as Wilf was being shouted at for leaving his shoes lying around and Ringo was being noisily sick in Ned's bed next to the radiator. Ned was hissing and arching his back in disgust and dancing around Ringo, taking a swipe at him every so often with needle-sharp claws.

'Now perhaps you can see why I don't want any more animals to look after?' Mum was saying. 'It's not as if that hen has even laid any eggs yet. If she doesn't lay one, I may have to change my mind about her staying, Wilfred.'

'I want to keep her,' Wilf pleaded.

'*I want to keep her*,' mimicked Meena.

'Grandma agrees,' said Wilf.

'*Grandma agrees*,' Meena whined.

'Oh, shut up,' said Wilf, turning on his sister.

'*Oh, shut up*,' said Meena.

'I am a stupid little girl,' said Wilf in a very challenging tone of voice.

Meena frowned and stuck her tongue out.

'Looks like I have arrived in the nick of time,' said Grandma.

CHAPTER 7

IF CATS MIGHT FLY

Once Wilf and Grandma had gone, Mum took Meena up to her room.

'Meena, darling,' she said. 'Your room is getting very messy. There is not enough room in here to swing a cat. Can you do something about it, please?'

'OK, Mummy,' Meena said sweetly.

Mum smiled indulgently. 'You are a good girl,' she said. 'I'll leave you to it then.' She left the room and went downstairs.

Meena waited until she was sure that Mum was out of earshot, then she muttered, 'Not enough room to swing a pussy-cat, eh?'

She went into Wilf's room and found Ned, who

had curled up on a pile of dirty laundry to enjoy a nap.

'Come to Meena,' she said, scooping him up. 'Meena needs your help.'

She carried the sleep-befuddled feline into her room, and before the poor animal could realize what was happening she had taken him by the tail and was spinning him round and round in circles, holding him out in front of her like a fat, furry kite.

'Raaaaooooooowww!' Ned howled, his legs flailing and his eyes bulging from their sockets.

Luckily for Ned, he was so heavy that Meena lost her grip almost immediately and he went flying through the air and crashed into the wall opposite, with a star-shaped 'splat'. Then he slid down the wall, his claws taking ribbons of wallpaper with them as he fell.

Meena giggled uncontrollably. 'Mummy was wrong. There is lots and lots of room to swing a pussy-cat in Meena's room,' she said.

Ned raced down the stairs and rocketed through the cat flap, leaving it hanging off its hinges. He normally did not even make it halfway through before getting stuck, but this time a surge of fear propelled him through and he whizzed across the lawn to safety.

Ringo raced after him and tried to fit through the broken cat flap too, but only succeeded in pulling the plastic frame completely away from the hole in the door, so that by the time Mum came in to see what all the noise was about Ringo was sitting on the floor, shaking his head in a bemused fashion to try to get the frame off from around his neck.

'Argh!' she cried. 'Ringo, you stupid, stupid dog!'

Meena slunk into the kitchen and said, her bottom lip trembling impressively, 'Don't be cross, Mummy.'

Mum immediately sank to her knees and enveloped her daughter in a hug. 'Oh, sweetie, I'm not cross with you! It's just the silly dog – look, he's broken the cat flap. I shall have to go and see if I've got anything in the shed to mend it with. Can you keep an eye on him in the garden while I do that?'

'Yes, Mummy,' said Meena. 'Come on, boy.'

She snatched a bottle of washing-up liquid from the sink and dragged Ringo out into the garden, leaving Mum muttering about 'the chaos these animals cause' and how if she had her way 'they would *all* go back to where they came from'.

'Come on, Ringo,' Meena cooed. 'Let's play.'

62

She mixed the washing-up liquid into Ringo's water bowl, which was by the back door.

'Have a nice drink, doggie,' she said, leading the Labrador to the bowl.

Ringo never bothered to stop and sniff anything before he ate or drank; consequently he wolfed the lot in a matter of seconds.

Very soon he was blowing bubbles out of his mouth, nose and ears. You might think this would be distressing for a dog – not Ringo. His tongue lolling out of the side of his mouth, he jumped and pounced with glee as the bubbles floated around the garden.

Meena was disappointed that Ringo was enjoying himself so much. She preferred it when her plans ended in chaos and misery.

'What can I do now?' she said to herself.

She looked over to the guinea pig's hutch, but considered how much Brian had freaked her out yesterday when he had bitten the milkman. The man's hand had bled quite a lot and Meena did not fancy being bitten herself by those sharp little teeth.

She thought instead about what she might do to the chicken.

Chickens are scratchy and pecky, though, she thought. I will have to think carefully before I decide what to do with her.

Meena went back inside to find that Mum had given up on the cat flap before she had even started. She was, in fact, back in her study on the computer.

'What are you doing, Mummy?' she asked, although she knew the answer already.

Mum looked round absent-mindedly. 'Oh, hello, darling. I'm just looking on the internet – I can't remember why I started now –' actually, she had been trying to find a demonstration of how to fix a broken cat flap, but had quickly been distracted by other things – 'but look at these *lovely* dresses. I was thinking I needed a new look. Why don't you help me choose, dear?'

Meena rolled her eyes. 'Don't care about stupid dresses and *new looks*,' she muttered. 'Mummy, Meena's bored!'

But Mum was engrossed in placing an order and did not seem to hear her.

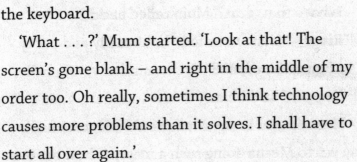

Meena crept up to the desk and pressed a button surreptitiously on the keyboard.

'What . . . ?' Mum started. 'Look at that! The screen's gone blank – and right in the middle of my order too. Oh really, sometimes I think technology causes more problems than it solves. I shall have to start all over again.'

'Mummy,' Meena began, 'if the 'puter is not workin', you can play instead?'

But Mum was already tapping furiously at the keys and talking to herself as she tried to find her order.

Meena scowled and ran to the kitchen, muttering under her breath, 'Stupid *new look*, stupid computer, stupid dresses. Mummy does not need a *new look* . . .'

Then she stopped. She looked through the window at Ringo, who was lying flat out on the lawn, panting with exhaustion from chasing all the bubbles he had created. He looked extremely bedraggled and smelly, Meena thought.

'Mu-um!' called Meena down the hallway. 'Pleeease can I give Ringo a baaath?'

'What's that, dear?' Mum called back.

'Ringo,' Meena repeated. 'He's smelly and yucky. Can I give him a bath?'

'Yes, yes,' said Mum.

Meena's eyes lit up. Mum would never normally say yes to Meena doing such a messy job on her own. That must mean that Mum was *really* distracted. But she *had* said yes . . . and an idea was forming in Meena's mind.

A *new look*. For Ringo.

'Thank you, Mummy,' she called in her sweetness-and-light voice. Then she smiled a nasty little smile to herself and skipped lightly back into the garden.

'Come on, Ringo!' she said. 'Good boy!'

Ringo jerked his head up at the sound of his name. He had been deeply asleep, but the sight of Meena grinning at him set his tail thumping, and he leaped up to follow her. It was always worth following Meena as she was the only one who fed him titbits from the breakfast table. Even if they were the sort of titbits that made him sick.

Meena led Ringo back into the kitchen. She climbed up on to a chair and from there she stepped on to a work surface so that she could fetch the dog treats down from one of the high cupboards.

'Here, boy!' she called to Ringo, dropping a treat on the floor.

While the Labrador gulped it down, Meena filled the washing-up bowl with hot water and a huge frothy mound of soapy suds. Then she soaked a large sponge in the water and jumped on to Ringo's back to hold him still. Ringo wheeled round in surprise just in time to receive a faceful of wet sponge. Meena rubbed his head briskly and then shoved a fist of dog treats into Ringo's mouth to keep him quiet while she covered the rest of him in soapy water. Once that was done, she grabbed a tea towel and dried him off. She threw another handful of treats in front of Ringo's nose and whisked open a drawer from which she produced a pair of kitchen scissors.

'Just a little trim,' she cooed as she began cutting great clumps of his fur off.

By this time, Ned had reappeared from his hiding place outside. He had observed the bubble-blowing incident from a safe distance, and had been worried that more Meena-style mischief was on the cards, so he had decided to keep an eye on her. Now he was watching Ringo's pooch-pampering session with growing alarm, his ears flat and his eyes wide. Much as he hated the dog, the sight of the poor dumb creature being attacked like this was more than he could bear. He launched himself at Meena with a howl, causing her to drop the scissors.

'What's going on?' Mum called from the study.

'Nothing, Mummy!' Meena assured her. 'I just been findin' a game to play.'

Then turning swiftly to Ned, she caught hold of him by the tail and whirled him round so that their noses were touching.

'Don't you dare drop me in it, buster,' she snarled softly. 'Or you will be next.'

CHAPTER 8

BIRDS OF A FEATHER

Ned shot out of the broken cat flap, a dark, black thunderbolt of feline fury. He made straight for Brian's hutch.

As he approached, he heard raised voices. Or, rather, raised squeaks and squawks.

'If I've told you once, I've told you a million times – you may NOT bring food into the bedroom! And if you think I'm going to put up with those sorts of toilet habits . . . Oh my, oh my, I think I'm having a panic attack—'

'You think YOU'RE having a panic attack? I think I'm having a nervous breakdown! Listen to me, you crazy tail-less rodent! I never asked to share my living arrangements with you—'

'Share YOUR living arrangements! Well, I like that! The presumption!'

'HEL-LO-O!' Ned shouted, pressing his face up against the wire of the guinea pig's run. 'I'm terribly sorry to interrupt what is clearly an incredibly *intellectual* debate, but I feel I must make you aware of something. It's a matter of extreme urgency,' he insisted.

Titch whirled round at the sound of his voice and let out a volley of alarmed clucking. 'It's the cat!' she squawked. 'The hairy monster who leaped at me and told me horrible stories to scare me and said I should get out if I knew what was good for me . . . if only I COULD get out of here. This place is a nightmare—'

'How dare you be so rude about my home!' shrieked Brian. 'And if you think the cat is a monster, just you wait. There's much worse out there in the garden at night, let me tell you. Foxes, for a start.'

'If you are trying to put me off escaping, you are

72

failing miserably—' Titch screeched.

'OH SHUT UP, THE PAIR OF YOU!' yelled Ned, arching his back and hissing at the chicken and the guinea pig. Being called a 'hairy monster' had done nothing to improve his mood.

The two animals took a step away from the cat and banged into each other. Ned stifled a snigger and said, 'That's better. We are no use against the enemy if we are fighting among ourselves.'

'Enemy?' squeaked Brian. 'What enemy?'

'For pity's sake!' howled Ned. 'If you would just let me finish.' He paused to fix the two creatures with a fierce stare. 'It's the Terror – the girl. She is up to her tricks again. I have come to warn you to lie low. She has been doing unspeakable things to me and Ringo again this morning. You may well be next, Brian. We don't want a repetition of the spin-dryer incident, now do we?'

'Oh, don't remind me!' Brian said, quivering. 'It took months for me to stop spinning round and round on the spot. I got dizzy just getting out of bed. Oh! It was dreadful—'

'Quite,' Ned cut in. 'And you would suffer far more if you were to experience what poor unfortunate Ringo has had to endure this morning.'

'The bubble blowing?' asked Brian.

'Worse,' said Ned. He went on to explain about Ringo's hair-cutting torture.

'But that's terrible!' Titch squawked.

'And she said you were next, Ned?' repeated Brian. 'That means I will be on her list too! Oh no, I'm having flashbacks! Do you remember the time she stuffed me in a cardboard tube and rolled me down a hill to see how fast I would go? Oh, my whiskers, oh, my sainted kernels of corn! Oh, my . . .' He began running round and round, squeaking hysterically as he went.

Ned yawned and said to Titch, 'I never thought I would say this, but I pity you having to share a house with this ball of neuroses.'

'A ball of what?' said Titch, looking round in panic. 'There's a ball of – of something or other horrible in here too? Oh, my feathers and claws! Oh, my—'

'You two are as bad as each other – birds of a feather in fact,' Ned quipped. He stopped suddenly and raised his head to listen. 'Oh no. We may be too late . . . I can hear her coming this way! Why on earth that useless mutt didn't retaliate I do not know. He's almost the same size as the Terror for heaven's sake. He could flatten her if he wanted.' Ned snarled in disgust. 'That hound will put up with anything if it means getting a bit of attention. Or food,' he added grimly.

Meena's voice could be heard quite clearly now, calling for Ned.

'Neddie! Where are you, naughty boy? Come to Meena!'

'Quick! Hide me!' hissed Ned.

'No way!' exclaimed Brian, burying himself in a mound of sawdust. 'I'm hiding myself, thank you very much.'

'I need time to hatch a plan,' said Titch. She was very flustered. She lowered her head and bustled to and fro as though she might find a plan lying around the floor of the hutch.

'Well, thanks for nothing,' said Ned. He turned to make his getaway.

But he was too late. A pair of small chubby hands had him round the middle and, struggle as he might, he could not escape.

Titch watched in horror as Meena lifted Ned up to her face and said in a voice as sharp as steel, 'No one runs away from Meena.' Then she looked at Titch with a particularly nasty grin and said, 'Watch out, chicky-wicky. I have plans for you too.'

CHAPTER 9

CAT-ASTROPHIC!

Meena carried the scratching, writhing Ned back to the house just as Mum came into the kitchen looking bleary-eyed from staring at the computer screen for so long. She went to make a cup of tea and looked over at Meena, who sat herself in the large armchair in the corner of the kitchen with Ned on her lap.

'You look snug,' said Mum, smiling weakly.

'Neddie-Weddie loves cuggles,' Meena cooed as she kept a tight hold on him.

'He does seem to,' Mum agreed. She yawned. 'Well, I've ordered some lovely summery dresses. I hope they are not too fancy. I'm not sure I can get away with fancy dresses at my age . . .'

'Fancy dress, Mummy?' Meena repeated. Another idea was already forming in her scheming mind.

Ned wriggled harder than ever.

'Not fancy-dress, darling!' Mum laughed. 'I definitely can't get away with that!'

'Meena thinks Mummy is beautiful in all her dresses,' Meena cooed.

Mum smiled and ruffled her daughter's golden hair. 'You are such a sweetheart. Where are you going with Ned?' she asked, eyeing the writhing cat.

'Neddie-Weddie is so cute that I'm going to give him a special ickle treat,' Meena continued, giving Mum a coy look.

'That's nice, dear,' said Mum with a sigh. 'And I think I might just have a little rest.'

'Yes, Mummy,' lisped Meena. 'I promise I'll be quiet.'

She slithered off the chair, still holding Ned in a vice-like grip, and carried the hissing bundle out of the room. She moved fast and quietly so as not to alert Mum to what she was up to.

78

Ned had a brief attempt at alerting Mum himself, but his miaow of distress was swiftly silenced by Meena, who was squashing his head into her jumper. She need not have bothered as Mum was already relaxing in her armchair, cradling her hot cup of tea in her hands.

'I think the pink one will suit me best,' she was saying. 'It'll go better with my complexion . . .'

'Come on, Neddie-Weddie,' Meena whispered into one flattened ear. 'I know just what will suit you.'

She scuttled upstairs to her bedroom and shut the door with her bottom. Only then did she let go of poor Ned, who immediately made a break for the bed to squeeze himself under it. Unfortunately for him, he did not fit. The last time he had tried this hiding place it had worked very well, but that is because it had been a long time ago when he was considerably smaller.

Meena laughed nastily. 'Neddie-Weddie needs to go on a diet,' she said.

Ned turned, drew back his lips and bared all his

79

teeth, letting out the most ferocious hiss he could manage. But it had no effect whatsoever on Meena, who merely drew back *her* lips, baring all *her* teeth (and all the gaps in between), and hissed even louder.

Ned flattened his ears against his head, arched his back and squashed himself into the side of the bed, as though hoping it might swallow him up or turn into some kind of transportation device that would take him away from the evil little girl advancing on him.

'Now, Neddie-Weddie, come on. Come to Meena,' she was saying, as she crept closer and closer.

'RAAAoooooooaaaaaAAW!' Ned howled as he was pounced upon.

There was a tussle and a flurry of claws, paws, fingers and elbows, then – 'Ta-daa!' Meena announced, stepping back to admire her handiwork.

Ned no longer looked like a cat. He looked like a stuffed toy (although a pretty angry stuffed toy, it has to be said). He was dressed in a hand-knitted

 80

jumper, which Grandma had made for one of
Meena's teddies, and a rather fetching skirt, which
Grandma had made from scraps of curtain fabric
for one of Meena's dolls. He had a woollen scarf
wrapped securely round his neck and on his head
was a bobble hat to match. Both these items had also
been knitted by Grandma. To finish the look, Ned
was sporting a colourful pair of wellie boots, kindly
donated by another of Meena's teddies.

'Awww, don't you look GORGEOUS,' cooed
Meena.

'Miaooow!' said Ned. He was most definitely not
in agreement.

'I'm going to take you out and show you off,' said
Meena.

Now you might be wondering why on earth Ned
didn't run away while he had the chance – and that
is a fair question. Most cats are extremely good
at escaping the grasp of the average human: they
seem to turn themselves to silk so that they can
slip and slither out of your grasp. But Meena was

not your average human. And, even if she was,
Ned was so trussed up in his ridiculous outfit that
any opportunity he'd had for wriggling, slipping or
slithering had long gone. Plus, have you ever seen a
cat running in wellies?

No, poor Ned was going nowhere. Meena had
already scooped him up and was cradling him like a
baby. She was singing soppy songs to him, and if you
had looked in through the window at that point you
might well have thought, Ah, how sweet: a little girl
playing with her dollies.

Meena hastily crammed Ned into her dolls' pram
and tucked the blanket tightly round him so that he
could not move at all.

'And now we're going for a walk,' she said.

She manoeuvred the pram out of her room and
on to the landing and then stopped at the top of the
stairs. She paused for a moment.

'Mmmm – how shall I do this?' she said aloud.

'Roaww?' Ned squeaked from under his blanket.

'Ah, that's it!' said Meena. 'I'll just give you a

teensy-weensy push.' And with that she kicked the pram hard.

It teetered for a moment on the top step and then – BE-DOM-BE-DOM-BE-DOM-BE-DOM! – it careered down the stairs at top speed.

Ned began to let out strangled cries of panic. His face would appear every time the pram went over a stair and then disappear as the pram bobbed down again. Once he had reached the bottom step, Ned had managed to free himself from the blanket, which had been loosened by the jolting movement of the pram, and as the pram hit the hallway and zoomed in the direction of the front door Ned was catapulted free and went whizzing through the air, losing the bobble hat in the process.

He landed on Ringo who had padded out into the hall in search of something to do.

'Aaaaieeeeee!' screamed Ned when he realized he was aiming straight for Ringo's nose.

'Ooouuuuwwww!' yelled Ringo, who had managed to duck, thus avoiding having his eyes gouged out,

but was nevertheless, thanks to Ned's extremely sharp front claws, now wearing a very spiky hat for the second time in as many days. He shook his head violently from side to side, and succeeded in dislodging Ned, who flew into the air again. This at least meant the rest of the dolls' clothes came off – all except the wellies, that is. Ned made a break for it, just as Mum came running from the sitting room to see what all the noise was about.

'Ringo! What are you up to now? OH! I have had it UP TO HERE with animals!' Mum shouted, holding her hand high above her head. She was far too cross to notice Ringo's odd new haircut.

She looked around. 'Meena?' she called. 'Meeeeennnaaaa! Where are you? Come and help Mummy, there's a dear.'

Meena was standing at the top of the stairs because that was the best spot from which to watch all the action. She had been grinning with delight at the mayhem she had caused, but now she put on her angel face and said softly, 'I'm here, Mummy.'

Mrs Peasbody looked up and saw a very scared little girl, cowering at the top of the stairs. 'Oh, poor Meena!' she exclaimed. 'Did the nasty dog frighten you?'

'Yes, Mummy,' whined Meena. 'And Ned. They went all scratchy and horrid and made scary noises. I was only tryin' to play wiv them.'

'Come here,' said Mum. 'I'll shut him out in the garden and you can come back into the study with me. Bad dog!' She shot Ringo a look of pure fury.

Ringo whimpered as if to say, 'It wasn't me!' and backed away as Meena came slowly down the stairs glaring at him.

Mum enfolded Meena in a comforting hug and crooned, 'Poor little girl.'

Meena snuffled and said, 'I was very frighted, Mummy.' Then she peered out from her mother's embrace at Ringo and narrowed her eyes into a look which very clearly said, 'I'm not done with you yet.'

CHAPTER 10
FREE AS A BIRD

Meena waited until Mum was settled back into her armchair, then she crept out of the house and made her way to Brian's hutch.

'Shall I have some fun with the guinea pig now?' she asked herself.

But Brian was rather boring: he wasn't greedy like Ringo, so you couldn't feed him Tangfastics and then watch him froth at the mouth. And he didn't have a tail or make lovely screechy, screamy noises like Ned did when you picked him up and swung him round.

Meena decided against the guinea pig and considered once more what it would be like to play with the Pekin.

'Hello, little chickie,' she cooed as she bent over the hutch. 'Are you having a nice time with that stupid boring Brian?'

With a careful glance over her shoulder to make sure that Mum was not watching, she opened the door and stuck her hand in, taking care to avoid Brian's sharp teeth. Luckily he seemed to have hidden himself away, leaving only Titch, pecking and scratching in the sawdust.

It was harder to catch the hen than Meena had thought it would be. Titch kept running over to the other side of the hutch, and occasionally used her wings to give herself some height so that she could evade Meena's grasp. Meena became more and more angry and frustrated with the little hen, whose cries of indignation and alarm were growing louder by the second.

'Come to Meena, chickie,' Meena wheedled in a sugary voice.

'Beeuruurrckk!' said Titch.

Meena growled. This really was hard work.

She was about to give up altogether when Titch suddenly gave an enormous squawk and launched herself at the nasty little girl's nose.

'Waaaah!' screamed Meena, toppling back and landing on her bottom just where Ringo had decided to go to the loo earlier that day. 'Urgh! Oh NOOOO! I'll get you for this!' she cried, hurling herself at the chicken.

But Titch had had a head start, and she was making the most of it. Free at last, she ran along the grass, head down, and opened her wings and flapped, then with a hop and a skip she took off and flew into the tree above Brian's hutch.

Meena jumped and snatched at the nearest branch, but she couldn't reach. This made her angrier than ever, and her jumping soon became stomping and her face became redder and redder until it actually looked as though her ears were letting off steam.

Brian had come out of his bedding where he had been hiding ever since Ned had come to warn him and Titch about Meena. He was clearly terrified by the noises that Meena was making and was staring at her, frozen in panic. Unfortunately for him, Meena saw him staring.

'WHAT ARE YOU LOOKING AT?' she snarled. She ran over to the hutch and stuck her hand in, grabbing poor Brian before he had a chance to think of hiding again. 'I'll teach you to laugh at me,' said Meena, hissing into the little creature's face. He definitely did not look as though he was laughing. He was shaking, in actual fact, and his dark shiny-button eyes were creased with fear. He squeaked and squeaked, but Meena had no pity.

'If the chickie won't play, Brian can play instead,' she said.

Later, once Meena had got bored of him and gone back inside, Brian began a desperate high-pitched squealing – the kind guinea pigs reserve for moments of acute emergency.

'Tiiiiiiitch – Tiiiiiiitch!' Brian was squealing.

90

'You have to help meeeee!'

Titch had no intention of helping whatsoever. She had achieved her ambition of escape, was no longer bound to share a home with an annoying rodent and felt as free as – well, as free as a bird should feel.

She peered down from the safety of her branch. 'I don't see what use a mere CHICKEN could be to you, Brian,' she said haughtily. 'I mean, I am a – what was it now? Oh, yes, that's right, "a good-for-nothing lazy layabout with no sense of pride in either my appearance or the state of my living quarters",' she finished, quoting Brian's angry words from an argument they'd had earlier that day.

'OOOHH!' Brian exclaimed. 'I'm sorry! I was far too hasty. Please forgive me. I'm sure we can come to some understanding if only you'll help me get out of this – whatever it is,' he said, looking down at himself.

Meena had surpassed herself this time. She had 'borrowed' a number of her mother's most colourful silk scarves and had swaddled Brian so that he looked like a very small, very furry baby Jesus in a nativity play. In fact, that seemed exactly the look she had been going for, as she had then lined a shoebox with straw and had placed Brian in the cardboard manger. It was a small box and the scarves were expertly and tightly wrapped. As a result, Brian was well and truly stuck.

Titch could not help a little chuckle at seeing Brian's predicament. 'You know, there is something very endearing about you all wrapped up like that with your cute little face peering up at me,' she chirped.

'Oh, for goodness sake, get me out of here!' cried Brian.

'I seem to remember saying the exact same thing to you only a few hours ago,' teased Titch. 'I don't know if I do want to help you. Now that I'm free, that's exactly how I wish to stay. If I get too close to you, I might end up being pounced on again by the Terror . . .'

'B-b-but even if you don't help me, you can't stay in the garden on your *own*!' cried Brian, struggling to free himself. 'You've seen how dangerous it is out in the big wide world – you'd have that awful girl to contend with, day in, day out. And what about the cat?'

'I don't see those are reasons *not* to try to escape,' said Titch. 'After all, look at you – the Terror reached into your hutch and captured you all too easily. No, I think that being out in the garden is a much safer place to be. I cannot be cornered out here. I can flap and fly to my heart's content.'

'That's what you think . . . !'

But whatever Brian was going to say next, he was prevented from doing so by a very upset Wilf, who had just come home to find his dog sporting an unattractive haircut, his cat still wearing wellies, his guinea pig swaddled up like a small furry baby Jesus . . .

'And look, Grandma!' he was shouting, tears pouring down his hot, angry face. 'Titch has been let out too!'

CHAPTER 11

AN EGGS-ASPERATING SITUATION

Wilf had been in such a good mood before he had witnessed the results of Meena's latest episode of mischief.

Grandma had met him from school with an announcement.

'I have discovered that there is going to be a poultry show in a couple of weeks' time!' she said.

'So?' Wilf had been a bit grumpy at first. He did not know what a pole tree show was, but it sounded rubbish. Who wanted to go to a show of poles and trees?

'You do know what a poultry show is, don't you, Wilf?' Grandma said kindly. 'It is a show for chickens and cockerels. And ducks and turkeys too, as a matter of fact – that's what "poultry" means.'

'Oh, THAT kind of pole tree show,' Wilf said, nodding wisely. 'Yeah. Course.'

He waited to see what Grandma would say next.

Grandma coughed and hid her mouth behind her hand. 'Well, I was thinking that you could take Titch. They have special classes for Pekins, and because she is a Lavender Pekin, and a very beautiful one, she might win a prize! Then even your mum will have to admit how special she is.'

Wilf's face lit up like a beacon. 'Grandma!' he cried. 'You are a genius. A GEE-NEE-USS!'

'I'm certainly no birdbrain,' Grandma said with a giggle.

'I can't wait to get home and tell Titch myself!' Wilf said, bouncing in his seat. He was happier and more excited than he had been in a long while.

But now Wilf was feeling anything but happy and excited. He had been appalled to see the state of his poor guinea pig, trussed up in all those scarves, and he had endured more than a few scratches while unwinding them from the wriggling creature. And, as if that was not bad enough, Wilf could not even see Titch now. She had disappeared into the foliage. He felt panic rising in his chest. It rose and rose until it came out of his mouth in a loud sob.

'N-n-now that Titch has escaped, how am I *ever* going to get a chance to take her to a show, Grandma?' he wailed.

Meena had come into the garden to watch the scene unfold. She wrapped her arms around Grandma's legs. 'Why is Wilfie cryin'?' she lisped.

'Not now, Meena dear,' said Grandma.

'But why is he cryin' like that? Doesn't he like his chickie to be free an' flyin' and happy?' Meena said, her blue eyes sparkling innocently.

Wilf glared at his sister through his tears.

'This is all your fault,' he snarled. 'It's always your fault. You ruin everything. I will make you pay for this.'

Meena raised her eyebrows at her brother to show that she doubted very much that he would make her pay. Then she stuck out her bottom lip and made her face go pink. 'Gran'maaaaaa! Wilfie's bein' HORRID!'

Grandma immediately swooped down and picked her up to give her a cuddle.

Wilf growled.

'Titch can't have gone far,' said Grandma in a soothing tone. 'Why don't you have a look around the garden for her, Wilf? I'll take Meena indoors with me – to keep her out of harm's way.' She said that last bit very pointedly, fixing her granddaughter with a look that clearly said 'I have got my eye on you, young missy'.

Wilf waited until his sister was safely inside and then rushed around the garden, looking under bushes, parting the leaves of shrubs, even hunting in plant pots. All to no avail.

He traipsed sadly back to Brian's hutch and plonked himself down on the grass, his head in his hands.

'Oh, Brian,' he said. 'How will I ever find Titch? And what if something nasty happens to her? Ned might get her . . .'

Brian shuffled up to the side of his hutch and pressed his face against the wire.

'Eeeeeeek!' he said. 'Eeeeeeeeeeeeek!'

The guinea pig seemed to be trying to say something. He was jumping up and down on his stumpy little legs and waving his front paws above his head.

Wilf glanced up and saw that Titch had re-emerged from her hiding place and was on a branch in the tree directly above Brian's hutch.

'Beuuurck!' said the little hen.

'Oh, Titch!' cried Wilf. 'It's all right, I'll save you.'

'Bueeeeuuuurrrrck!' said Titch. She did not sound as though she wanted to be saved. She had puffed her chest out and was looking down in a haughty manner on both the boy and the guinea pig.

'Eeeeeeeek!' Brian said, looking up at the hen. He seemed rather cross, Wilf thought.

Wilf had an idea. He left his guinea pig and the hen hurling insults at each other and ran to the garden shed to get his butterfly net. He loved collecting butterflies in it so that he could make lists of all the different kinds he found. He always set them free again, though, because that's the kind of thoughtful boy he was.

He grabbed the net, which was very large and very soft, so as not to damage butterflies' wings. Then he launched himself at Titch, throwing the net high while she was busy arguing with Brian.

Brian was telling the hen what a fool she was to stay out in the wilds of the garden on her own. Titch retorted that she was not a lily-livered ball of fluff like him and she could look after herself.

All in all, it was probably a good thing that Wilf could not understand his pets. He might not have liked them so much if he knew what they were really saying.

Wilf was having trouble with the net. Try as he might to reach Titch, even by jumping and leaping, he was not tall enough.

'Help me!' he wailed uselessly, for there was no one there to come to his aid.

Then he plonked himself down on the grass and buried his head in his hands for the second time that afternoon. His brain was a boiling pot of anxious thoughts. What if Titch never came down? What if she flew further and further from tree to tree, and found her way out of the garden?

He could not lose her, not so soon after getting her.

CHAPTER 12

FEELING FLIGHTY

Meena was sitting on the floor by the radiator. She had been busy poking cheese down the back of it while Grandma helped Mum with the tea, but she looked up when she heard her brother's distress.

'Please, Grandma!' Wilf was saying. 'You've *got* to help.'

Grandma shook her head sorrowfully. 'I'm sorry, Wilfie. I am too old to jump up and down with a butterfly net. I think we should wait a little while longer. We know Titch can fly, so I'm sure she'll come down of her own accord.'

'But what if she doesn't!' Wilf groaned. He let his arms fall to his sides and flopped his head back to demonstrate how hopeless the whole situation was.

Mum came into the room to see what the fuss was about.

Ringo came in with her and immediately sniffed out the melting cheese and went to slurp it up.

'Have you found the hen?' Mum asked.

Wilf nodded sorrowfully. 'She's stuck up a tree.'

'Don't worry, dear,' said Grandma. 'Hens really do not like to stay out at night, you know. They like to come home to roost. So I think we should leave her be. I'm sure all the *fuss* has made her feel . . . flighty.' She paused to let her comment sink in 'She will find her own way back to the hutch, I'm sure.'

'But I can't leave the hutch door open cos then *Brian* will escape too!' Wilf exclaimed.

Meena came over to Grandma and climbed on to her lap. 'Can Brian come in the house, Gran'ma?' she asked sweetly.

Mum frowned. 'I don't know about that . . .'

Grandma shot Mum a look. 'It's not a bad idea, you know.'

Meena clapped her hands. 'Yay! Bagsy Meena give Brian a snuggle.'

Wilf narrowed his eyes. '*You* are not going *anywhere* near him,' he growled.

Grandma laid a hand on her grandson's shoulder. 'Now, now,' she said. 'I think Meena's right. Brian looked as though he could do with a cuddle. We'll bring him in, keep him in a cardboard box in the kitchen while we are having tea and then we'll go and check on Titch before bedtime.'

Mum sighed noisily. 'I really don't think—' But she was interrupted by Ringo, who had eaten rather a lot of radiator fluff with the melted cheese and was now being noisily sick on the floor at Mum's feet. 'DOH!' she shouted. 'This is precisely why I do not like ANIMALS IN MY HOUSE!'

'I'll clear that up,' said Grandma. Then she turned to Wilf. 'Go and get Brian,' she said quietly. 'I'll deal with your mother.'

Wilf went back out into the garden. 'Poor Brian,'

he said, eyeing the quivering guinea pig. 'You don't look very happy.'

'Eeeeeeek!' said Brian.

'I know,' said Wilf. 'I would not be happy either if I'd had the day you've had. You were probably frightened about Titch flying away, weren't you?'

'Eeeeek!' said Brian.

Wilf cradled him close and mumbled softly to him as he carried him in. Brian seemed to like that and had soon calmed down and snuggled into the crook of Wilf's arm.

When Wilf came up to the house, Grandma was by the back door, washing out the bucket of cheesy dog sick. Wilf wrinkled his nose.

'Ah, he looks happier already,' said Grandma, seeing Brian snuggled in Wilf's arms. 'Let's go and find him a nice box, shall we?'

'What if Titch doesn't realize the hutch is her home yet?' Wilf asked as he followed Grandma inside. He could not bear the thought of the little hen being alone in the garden all night.

105

Grandma turned round to give Wilf a quick hug and was careful not to squash Brian. 'Don't worry,' she said. 'Chickens are a lot more intelligent than we give them credit for. A lot goes on inside that tiny brain of theirs.'

'Miaaaaoow,' said Ned, who was following.

Wilf glanced over his shoulder at the cat. 'Ned doesn't sound as though he agrees with you, Grandma.'

Grandma smiled. 'What does he know?' she said.

Ned hissed.

Wilf gave a shuddery sigh. 'S'pose,' he said.

Grandma was right about most things, in his experience. He only hoped she was right this time too.

Later, Grandma was chopping carrots and Mum was reading a magazine while she stirred a sauce absent-mindedly. Meena was hovering around Mum and sticking her tongue out at Wilf whenever she was sure no one was looking.

'You are the most horrible sister in the whole,

entire universe,' Wilf whispered. 'How could you *do* those things to my pets? That was Cruelty to Animals, you realize,' he added.

'OooOO,' Meena whispered back. 'I'm *so* scared,' she added, with an extravagant eye roll, to show that she was anything but. Then she came right up to Wilf and hissed, 'In any case, they are not *your* pets. They are *everyone's* pets. And it wasn't Cruelty to Animals, it was only Cruelty to Ned. Brian and Ringo did not mind what I did –' Brian shuffled nervously in Wilf's arms – 'only Ned made a fuss. And Ned deserves it. He scratches. And he is nasty to mice and voles and things.'

Wilf went red. 'That's his job, stupid.'

'His *job*?' scoffed Meena. 'Cats don't have *jobs*. You are mental, *Wilfie*.'

'Better to be mental than evil,' snapped Wilf.

'Mummeeeeee!' Meena complained, her most annoying baby voice rising in volume. 'Wilfie's bein' horrid to Meena, again.' She crossed her arms dramatically.

'And Meena's been taking poor Brian out of his hutch and dressing him up,' Wilf said.

'Eek! Eeek!' said Brian.

Meena pouted and looked very hurt indeed. 'Have not. Wilfie's lyin',' she said in her most babyish voice. 'I was playing wiv my dollies.'

Mum tutted. 'Can't you see I'm busy, Wilf dear?' she said, without looking up. 'I don't think you would do such a nasty thing as that to Brian, would you, Meena?'

'No, Mummy,' Meena assured her. 'I love Brian.'

'Eeeeeek!' said Brian.

Wilf looked down and saw the guinea pig's eyes were wide with fear.

'Actually,' Grandma began, 'when we got home from school, Brian was wearing an interesting array of—'

'See, Wilfie?' said Mum, gesturing to Meena and ignoring Grandma. 'Meena loves Brian. So there's no need to make up stories.' She continued stirring the sauce on the hob and reading her magazine. She had been engrossed in an article about a new anti-wrinkle gel. She was thinking about how all the stress in her life had given her so many wrinkles. She remembered that she had placed a bulk order for some anti-wrinkle gel online a while ago, but it had been a disaster as she had gone on to the wrong site and had ended up with boxes and boxes of fruit jelly instead.

I really must return that jelly, she thought to herself as she set about putting Ned's food into his bowl, which was ready and waiting on the work surface. I don't want Meena to find it. Ever since a nasty child put some down the back of her neck at a birthday party she hasn't been able to stand the stuff. I wonder where I put the returns label?

'MUM!' Wilf shouted. 'Look at what you are doing!'

Mrs Peasbody looked up at her son distractedly. 'Look at what, dear?' she said.

'Cat food!' Wilf cried, pointing at the pan of sauce. 'You've just put Ned's food in our tea!'

'Oh, honestly,' Mum tutted. She picked up the pan and began scraping the cat food from it into Ned's bowl, sauce and all. 'Did you move the cat's bowl, Wilfred? I was sure I had put it right here. I have to have eyes in the back of my head with you, don't I, young man? I shall have to start all over again now! Oh, I can't be bothered. We'll have to have boiled eggs instead.'

Meena sniggered, but when Wilf glanced back at her she looked up and made her eyes wide in a picture of innocence.

'Talking of eggs, is there any danger of that hen of yours actually laying any?' Mum asked.

Wilf frowned. 'Not now she is up a tree . . .'

 110

'Because,' Mum went on, ignoring him, 'I would be a lot keener on having her as a pet if she did, you know.'

'And if she doesn't lay any, Mummy,' Meena said, 'you are getting rid of her, aren't you? That's what you said.' She shot a sly look at her distressed brother, who was shaking his head vehemently.

'What's that, dear?' Mum asked.

Wilf noted with relief that his mother had gone back to reading the magazine, so had not heard what Meena had said. He narrowed his eyes and pointed at his sister while mouthing the words, 'I'm watching you.'

'And I'm watching *you*,' Meena mouthed back.

CHAPTER 13

FLOWN THE NEST

Grandma had suggested they place Brian in an open-topped cardboard box in the sitting room near the radiator. (The radiator in the kitchen still smelt cheesy.) She told Wilf that the warmth would help Brian to stop shivering. He was still shaking after his ordeal with Meena and his argument with Titch, but Grandma of course thought it was because he was cold.

Brian very much appreciated the kindness that Wilf and Grandma showed him. He also appreciated Grandma staying in the room with him while she drank her cup of tea, as he was not convinced that Meena would not try more of her nasty tricks on him, given half a chance. He was feeling comfortable again for the first time in a couple of days: Grandma and Wilf had filled the box with fresh, sweet-smelling bedding and had put down a water pot and food pot in the far corner, just as he liked it. Also, it was nice and cosy here next to the radiator. His tummy was full and his bed was looking very inviting indeed. He gave a happy squeak and burrowed into the bedding until it was exactly how he always had it. He was just nodding off when a smooth, familiar voice made him jump.

'Brian . . . Brian! Don't go to sleep! We have important things to discuss.'

Brian felt his throat tighten. He had never trusted that cat.

'Eeeeeeek!' he squealed. 'What do you want? I'm in more danger here than I was outside, aren't I? That's what you're going to tell me. Oh no! What if I never see my beautiful hutch ever again? What if this is part of some sinister plot on behalf of that flappy chicken to get me rehoused . . . ?'

'Will you please stop that wretched squeaking and listen to me for one second?' Ned hissed. 'I am not going to hurt you, for heaven's sake. In fact, I was rather hoping I could persuade you – and the hen, if she ever comes back – to help me out.'

Brian quivered, but he did as he was told. Something in Ned's tone told him the cat was in earnest. He peeped timidly out of his sawdust duvet.

'What do you have in mind?' he asked.

Ned checked that Grandma was not watching. Then he leaned in closer and said quietly, 'I want you to help me get my own back on that insufferable girl.' He flicked his head towards the kitchen. 'She has been making my life a misery for years and I have been looking for an opportunity to teach her a lesson. Today has been a nightmare from start to finish. And that dressing-up stint was the last straw. The humiliation! Her time has come, let me tell you.'

'What do you mean . . . ?'

'In a word,' said the cat, 'revenge.'

*

Meanwhile Wilf was feeling more and more miserable.

'Titch hasn't found her way home yet and it's getting dark,' he said. 'And Mum says it's good riddance because she never wanted Titch anyway and she hasn't laid any eggs, so she is a "good-for-nothing birdbrain"!' His eyes were wide with alarm, his little freckled face pale in the evening gloom. 'I've looked everywhere, Grandma,' he went on. 'I took my head torch and I looked under all the bushes and shrubs. I think – I think something must've got her!'

Grandma took Wilf by the shoulders. 'Don't despair,' she said firmly. 'She must be out there somewhere. I'll help you look.'

She shot an anxious glance at Ned who seemed to be prowling around Brian's cardboard box. 'I think we should take Brian back out to his hutch while we're at it.'

Wilf glanced across at the animals. It's not Ned you have to be worried about in this house, he thought.

They picked up Brian, took their coats off the pegs

by the back door and went out into the garden with a big torch, which Grandma said would be better than only a head torch to guide them.

Once the guinea pig had been returned to his hutch, Wilf and Grandma searched high, low and in between. They looked underneath and in the middle of every place in the garden they could think of. They looked in the greenhouse and in the garden shed. They even hunted in the compost heap and the bonfire pile. But Titch was nowhere to be seen.

Wilf was in tears now. He knelt down by Brian's hutch and whispered, 'Oh, where did she go, Brian? Can't you tell me?'

Brian squeaked and squeaked and dug himself deeper into his bed of sawdust and sat there, his pink nose quivering, as though he was feeling very sorry for himself (which, of course, he was).

'Wilf, love, I think we should go in.' Grandma had come up to the hutch and was crouched down, listening to her grandson talking to his guinea pig. 'I'm not sure there's much more we can do tonight.

Come on, we'll make a plan of action for tomorrow.'

Wilf got up slowly and wiped his eyes on the back of his sleeve. 'I don't want anything to happen to her!' he sniffed.

'I know,' said Grandma.

'I wanted to take her to that pole tree show,' he went on.

'And you will,' said Grandma.

But Wilf did not think she sounded very sure about that.

CHAPTER 14

FREE-RANGE CHICKEN

Brian was finally dozing off when he heard a scratching noise on the other side of his bedroom wall.

He jerked awake and held his breath as he tried to work out what it was. Surely the Terror would not come out in the dark?

'Brian?' said a voice.

It didn't sound like the Terror. It didn't sound like the cat either.

Scratch, scratch, scratch.

'Brian! You dozy little—'

'T-Titch?' said Brian. 'Is that you?'

'Who else would it be?' said the hen.

'You could be anyone! You could be Ned in disguise. You could be a rat! Rats spread germs. I have enough problems without germs!' Brian squeaked. 'I've probably already got bird flu anyway, thanks to you—'

'Oh, for goodness sake,' clucked Titch. 'Forget it. I only came to say goodbye.'

Brian shuffled out of his bedroom and peered into the darkness. 'So, it really is you.' He sounded almost disappointed. 'Well, I – I can't let you in. Wilf and Grandma have gone and I can't undo the door. You know that. You're going to have to stay out all night!' The guinea pig hurled himself at the wire mesh to demonstrate the hopelessness of the situation. 'Look! It's solid! I can't break it down! Oh no, what are we going to do?' He was winding himself up into a full-scale panic attack. 'This is all my fault, isn't it? If I had been kinder, if I had shared my food, if I hadn't shouted at you . . . I'm sorry. I'm—'

'Be quiet!' Titch chirruped. 'You'll let the whole garden know I'm out here. Listen, I *wanted* to escape,

119

didn't I? I keep telling you, I don't belong here. I deserve to be wandering free range, out in the fields and the woods, making a life for myself, doing something marvellous! I spent enough of my life hemmed in while I was in the chicken run. I'm sorry, Brian. There's a whole world out there, and I intend to see it.'

'In the middle of the *night*?' squealed Brian. 'But you can't see anything at all – it's pitch black!'

'Aha, but that is where you are wrong,' said Titch. There was a small click and the hutch was flooded with light.

'Waaah! What's that?'

Titch's voice came from behind the light. 'A head torch. Wilf dropped it when he was out looking for me earlier.'

120

Brian picked up a piece of corn and began nibbling at it nervously. 'I – I need to tell you something about Out There,' he squeaked.

Titch clucked impatiently. 'What on earth could you tell me that would be of any use to me whatsoever? You never go anywhere unless you are lifted out by that horrible little girl. I doubt you even know what is at the bottom of the garden, let alone what lies beyond.'

The piece of corn got stuck in Brian's throat and set off a nasty coughing fit. 'Wait!' he shrieked as Titch began backing away. 'I need – craaauuugghh – to tell – blerurrugh – you!' He eventually managed to dislodge the corn. 'I need to tell you about THE MONSTER!'

She laughed. 'There is no monster – it's only Ned. I've worked that one out for myself.'

'No, no!' Brian insisted. 'Ned is the least of your worries. Trust me, you do not want to be out in the garden after dark. There are animals far worse than Ned to contend with. I tried telling you this earlier,

121

but you will not listen, will you? Have you ever met a fox—?'

'You, Brian, are a nervous wreck!' Titch cut in impatiently. 'The only thing to fear is fear itself. I am going to prove it by going on an adventure. And if you are lucky I shall come back to visit you one day and I'll tell you all about how marvellous it has been!'

Brian stopped chewing for a moment and put his head on one side. 'You would come back and visit me?' he asked shyly.

'Yes, yes,' Titch chirruped. 'But first I am going to do a spot of reconnaissance.'

'What's that?' squeaked Brian in alarm. 'It sounds terrifying!'

Titch fluffed her feathers out and clucked. 'It simply means that I want to take a good look around to plan my escape route. It's what all clever spy types do, you know. I need to keep the area under surveillance.'

'Surveillance? Escape route? Since when were you

a spy?' Brian twittered. 'I thought you wanted to roam free and do "something marvellous"? Now all of a sudden you are a *spy*?'

But Titch was already moving away from the door. 'I can't hang around here all night,' she said. 'I'm a chicken on a mission. And anyway, you should get some sleep. It's bad for your nerves to stay up all night.'

But the little hen did not feel so brave once Brian had retired, squeaking irritably, to his sleeping quarters. Suddenly the garden seemed darker than before, and the air was alive with strange noises.

'Wooo-wooo!'

Titch leaped into the air in fright. It was all she could do to stop herself from squawking. 'Now don't go getting into a flap,' she told herself sternly. 'It's all the fault of that Brian, filling your head with his stupid ideas.'

'Sschhhhrrrrrreeeek!'

'Oh, my goodness, oh, my goodness!' Titch

chirruped. She scuttled under the nearest bush and huddled down, shivering. 'This was probably one of the stupidest ideas I have ever had! But it's too late for regrets,' she said, trying to make herself feel brave again. 'And I can't have that tail-less rat telling me "I told you so". I need to keep my wits about me while I suss out the lie of the land.'

She took a deep breath and stuck her head out of

the bush. A bright light suddenly flooded the garden, which nearly made Titch squawk again. But then she looked up and realized where it was coming from.

'Now you really are being silly,' she told herself. 'That must be the moon! I remember some of the girls in the chicken run telling stories about it. How beautiful and silvery it was. At last I get to see it for myself instead of being shut in all night.' She sighed. Then, turning to more practical matters, 'And the good news is, I won't have to use this stupid torch to see by any more.' She gave a swift kung-fu style kick at the switch and turned the torch off.

Titch looked about her, mesmerized by the beauty of the garden. The trees and grass were glowing, and the windows of the house shone like mirrors. As Titch let her eyes become accustomed to this new kind of light, she saw that there were thousands of stars out there in the sky as well.

'This is the life!' she cooed. 'This is why I had to get out. There is a whole world to see and I am not going to miss it.'

She crept out from under the bush and tiptoed quietly into the middle of the lawn.

'Where shall I go? I could fly up on to the roof and

have a bird's-eye view from there,' she said.

She lowered her head, took a run-up and opened her wings as wide as she could, her little feet pounding the grass faster than they ever had before. Then she closed her eyes for the lift-off and flapped and flapped as hard as she could.

'Would you like a hand?' said a smooth voice from somewhere in the shadows.

'Oh!' cried Titch, coming back down to earth with a bump. She whirled round and flung her claws out, just to be on the safe side.

'Dear me, madam,' said the voice. 'There's no need to be so prickly. I was only being friendly. Although I apologize for alarming you. I must admit that the moonlight plays terrible tricks, does it not? Perhaps you cannot see me clearly.' With those words, there was a rustling of leaves and a sleek, handsome face appeared in a gap in the hedge.

Titch felt rather ashamed of herself. All that talk of being brave and the only thing to fear being fear itself, and here she was getting terribly flighty – and being rude to an extremely polite and good-looking stranger.

'I – I am terribly sorry,' she twittered, fluffing out her feathery petticoats and bobbing a little curtsy. 'I don't know what came over me.'

The stranger bowed his head graciously. 'That is quite all right. One never knows whom one might meet out and about on a night like this, but I can assure you, you have nothing to be scared of.'

And with that he stepped fully out of the shadows and gave a deep bow and a swish of his fine tail.

Titch did not mind admitting to herself that she was speechless. This was not something that had happened many times in her short life, but then again, she had never met anyone so debonair, so beguiling, so handsome.

The gentleman smiled and licked his lips. 'What a perfectly *delicious* little creature you are,' he said with a drawl. 'Would you care to take a stroll through the garden with me?'

'Oh – y-yes,' said Titch.

'Oh NO, more like!' said a voice.

The attractive stranger whirled round, but his reaction was too slow. With a screeching war cry, a black-caped crusader (or so it seemed to Titch) had landed on his shoulders.

'Gerroff! Gerroff!' shouted the stranger, sounding decidedly less suave now that he was under attack. He leaped and twirled and swiped at the figure, but to no avail. 'Get your claws off me!'

'Only if you promise to leave right this instant,' hissed the voice.

Titch was flapping in circles, clucking and chirping. If she had calmed down for just one instant, she might have realized that the voice belonged to someone she knew, but all she could think was, I have to get to safety! I have to hide somewhere!

'All right, all right,' said the stranger. 'But this is just not cricket, you know. It's finders keepers in my book. And I found her first.'

'Yes, well, I think you'll find this is a case of losers weepers, mate,' said the voice. And there was another howl from the stranger as his attacker sank his claws in deeper to prove his point.

'I'm going, I'm going!' cried the stranger. And with that he gave a final shake to rid himself of his assailant, and melted silently into the bushes from where he had come.

CHAPTER 15

OUT OF THE FRYING PAN . . .

'Oh my!' said Titch. 'Please don't hurt me, please don't—'

'It's me, you fool,' said the voice.

Titch peered at the dark figure, and then remembered her torch. She kicked at it and switched it back on.

'Turn it off! For heaven's sake, do you want to announce your presence to the whole garden? It's not just foxes you have to careful of, birdbrain!'

'Ned?' exclaimed Titch. 'Is that really you?'

'Who else did you think it would be?' said the cat. 'The Queen?' He waved a paw crossly towards the torch and repeated, 'Turn it off!'

Titch did as she was told and let her eyes become accustomed to the moonlight again. Then she said cautiously, 'What was that you said about – foxes?'

Titch had heard tales of foxes in the chicken run, of course. Terrible creatures, they were said to be, with needle-sharp teeth and razor-like claws, who liked nothing better than to tear a chicken limb from limb just for the fun of it. She shivered. 'Are there really foxes? Here? In this garden? I thought that was just Brian telling me stories to unnerve me.'

Ned rolled his large yellow eyes. 'Who the devil did you think that was you were talking to just then? Father Christmas?'

'The devil? Father Christmas? I don't know what you are talking about!' twittered Titch.

'Hmm, I can see that,' said Ned. He washed one paw thoughtfully. 'Where did you live before you came here?' he asked.

Titch bristled. 'I don't see what that has to do with anything,' she said.

Ned let out a short, sharp derisive miaow. 'It has

everything to do with *everything*!' he declared. 'You are hardly a chicken of the world. You say that you want to escape, to do "something marvellous" . . .' He tailed off with a sneer.

'Hey!' Titch protested.

'So, I've been listening in,' Ned said, waving his paw dismissively. 'It's not hard. You and Brian make a noise fit to rouse a hedgehog from hibernation.'

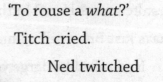

'To rouse a *what*?' Titch cried.

Ned twitched his whiskers in amusement.

'You don't know what a *hedgehog* is either?' He cleared his throat and in a droning, teacherly voice said, 'A hedgehog is any of the spiny mammals of the subfamily *Erinaceinae*, which is in the order *Erinaceomorpha*. There are seventeen species of hedgehog in five genera . . .'

'Oh, shut up,' said Titch.

Ned started. 'Charming,' he said. 'You really are a bird of very little brain. And you don't get out much, do you?'

'I am out *here* tonight,' said Titch huffily. 'And I'm going to *stay* out. I cannot remain with that tail-less rat a moment longer.'

Ned flicked his own long and fluffy tail. His mouth twisted once more into a look of amusement, but he persisted. 'That's all very well, but you simply have no idea of the dangers you will face. That creature reeling you in with his charming ways and silky smooth voice back there – *that*, my feathered friend, was a fox. A real live one!' At this, poor Titch became flappier than ever. 'You see?' Ned continued. 'Your reaction plainly tells me that you know what foxes do to chickens. But you had evidently never come across one before, or you would have taken flight the moment you saw him.'

Titch gave a fluttery sigh and flopped down on to the silvery, dewy grass. 'You're right,' she said. 'I know nothing about anything and I've never been

133

outside a chicken run in my life – before coming here, I mean. I lived in a large enclosure with so many other chickens I had no idea how many there were. I did not even know all their names. It was intolerable! I know I've painted quite a different picture to you all, but I could see you had freedoms I had only dreamed of. I felt pathetic in comparison. I have spent my whole life imagining what it would be like to roam the fields and hedgerows the older hens told us about in their bedtime stories.'

'I see,' said Ned. 'So how *did* you escape?'

'There was a rumour going round that some of us were going to be sent to new homes. The other hens were suspicious and did not want to be moved so they ran around the run clucking and flapping and causing a hullaballoo. But I thought, If only I can get out of the run, I can use it as the first stage in an escape into the wider world. So when I saw the farmer coming with some boxes, I sat very, very still so that I was easy to pick up.'

Ned was impressed. 'That was extremely

courageous of you,' he said. 'You had no idea of your destination?'

'None at all,' said Titch. 'And I am now beginning to regret my actions. It seems I have left the frying pan only to find myself in the fire! I need to get out of here, Ned. I need to make the most of my life – you only get one chance to do something marvellous. Sharing a home with that bossy little Brian is even more unbearable than living with hundreds of other chickens. And as for those children: well, the boy is quite sweet, I know. But the girl—'

'Yes, don't get me started on the girl,' Ned cut in. 'She is not known as the Terror for nothing; she's every bit as much a menace as the fox. Possibly more so. However, have no fear. I have a plan for dealing with her. But that will have to wait. If we don't get you to safety, you will not survive the night. I am afraid you are not going to like this, but I feel sure you would be better off going back to your home – to *Brian's* home,' he corrected himself, 'just until you have thought your escape plan through a bit more carefully.'

'I can't! It's impossible!' Titch began.

'You will have to,' Ned said firmly. 'There are badgers as well as foxes out here – who knows what else might be on the prowl.'

'How do I know I can trust *you*?' Titch asked suddenly. She backed away as Ned stalked towards her. 'What if *you* are the dangerous one, not the fox? What if you have been spinning me a pack of lies, befuddling me with all your clever language and wily ways, just so that you can lure me into your den, or . . . whatever,' she added vaguely. She realized she had no idea where the cat actually lived.

Ned snorted. 'I don't have a DEN,' he said. 'I live in the house with the family and that excuse for an animal they call Ringo, more's the pity. And if I had wanted to hurt you let me tell you I could have done it a million times by now. I could have pounced on you while you were flirting with the fox.'

Titch thought about this for a second and realized it was probably true. 'All right,' she said. Then she added grudgingly, 'I suppose this means I owe you my life. You saved me from the fox. But, if I'm honest, I don't understand why you bothered. What's in it for you?'

Ned fixed her with his flashing yellow eyes and said, 'You say you want to do something marvellous? Well, you can start, my flighty friend, by helping me, Ringo and Brian get our own back on the Terror.'

CHAPTER 16

AN UN-EGGS-PECK-TED PARCEL

'What we need to do is find her Achilles heel,' Ned
said, once he and Titch were back in Brian's hutch.
Ned had proved himself quite a dab paw at opening
the door, much to Brian's consternation.

'What are you talking about? A killer what?'
squealed Brian. 'I don't like the sound of that at all.'
And he began scurrying around in ever decreasing
circles, kicking up chunks of sawdust, which made
Titch sneeze.

Ned sat patiently, washing his paws and yawning.
Finally he said, 'When you have quite finished
working yourself into a frenzy, we will explain.'

Brian screeched to a halt, sticking his paws out in

138

front of him. They acted like a mini snow-plough, causing a mountain of sawdust to pile up in front of him. Titch had to look away to stop herself from giggling.

Ned coughed and said, 'All right now?'

Brian nodded nervously and sat down.

'So, as I was saying, we need to find the Terror's Achilles heel, which is another way of saying that we need to find her weak spot. You see Achilles was a Greek hero whose mother dipped him into a magic pool to prevent him from being killed in battle, but she forgot to dip his heel in so—'

'I don't think we need a history lesson,' said Titch sharply.

'I think you'll find you need lessons in more than just history,' Ned muttered. 'I can see why they put you in with Brian. Birds of a feather flock together.'

'I do NOT have feathers!' Brian squeaked. 'These are rosettes!' He preened himself indignantly.

'I thought we had arranged a meeting to discuss the Terror,' chirruped Titch.

'And so we have,' said Ned. 'I propose that I follow her at all times to find out what it is that frightens her the most,' he went on. 'And then the next time she tries to kidnap one of us we will be ready to pounce.'

'Call that a plan?' Brian complained. 'There's no detail, no idea of how you will attack. You haven't got the faintest clue, have you? In any case, we've been here before – she is not frightened of anything! That is the point! She is a devil! A monster!'

Titch sniffed. 'I thought the fox was the monster?' She scratched at the floor of the hutch to call the meeting to order. 'Brian,' she said, her head on one side in a patronizing manner, 'this is only the

 140

brainstorming session. We are throwing our ideas into the air to see what we come up with.'

'Listen!' Ned interrupted. 'Why don't you let me do a spot of spying and I'll report back.'

'No way,' said Titch. 'If anyone is going to be doing any spying around here, it'll be me.'

Ned looked at her doubtfully. 'Now that you are back in with Brian, I don't think that you will be going anywhere, do you?' he said. He yawned again and stretched luxuriously. 'Anyway, it's nearly daybreak. I must be going. I'll let you know how I get on. As my French cousins would say, *Au revoir, mes amis*.'

And with a flick of his tail, he was gone.

Back in the house Wilf was waking up. He had slept fitfully, his rest broken by bad dreams concerning lost chickens dressed as dolls flying through the night sky, and his sister's face looming over him, laughing like a mad witch.

He woke properly with a start as the grey fingers

of dawn reached through under his curtains and tweaked at his duvet.

Actually it was Ned doing the tweaking: he had jumped on to Wilf's head and was now purring loudly in his ear.

'Ne-ed,' Wilf complained blearily. 'I'm . . . sleeping . . . Oh! It's morning. I must go and check the garden for Titch.'

'Miaaaow,' said Ned, landing heavily on the carpet.

Wilf scrambled out of his twisted duvet, hastily pulled a jumper on over his pyjamas and took a pair of the day-before-yesterday's socks from the ever-expanding pile of dirty laundry in the middle of the room. He tiptoed into the corridor so that he did not wake anyone (especially Meena) and crept down the stairs with Ned padding softly behind.

Grandma was already in the kitchen making herself a cup of tea. She smiled when Wilf came in. 'Couldn't sleep?' she asked.

Wilf shook his head.

'Still worried about Titch?' she said.

Wilf nodded and made for the back door.

'There's no need,' said Grandma. 'She's back.'

Wilf's face split into a grin so wide it looked as though someone had taken hold of his ears and pulled them to make his face go stretchy. He punched the air and whooped for joy, raced to get his wellies, then ran out to Brian's hutch.

Grandma followed at a more steady pace, but she was beaming too.

They bent over the hutch together and watched as Titch bustled about, pecking and scratching as though she had never been away. Brian squeaked at her from his bed corner.

'Look at them,' said Grandma. 'Like an old married couple.'

Wilf scoffed. 'I don't think Titch would want to marry a guinea pig, Grandma.'

Grandma laughed. 'She might want to enter this, though,' she said, fetching a crumpled piece of paper from out of her pocket.

'The pole tree show!' shouted Wilf. 'Yay!'

'My thoughts exactly,' said Grandma. 'Now let's talk about what we need to prepare for the show while we have a bit of peace and quiet.'

The peace and quiet did not last long enough for Wilf's liking. He had been enjoying having Grandma to himself and dreaming about how Titch would win a prize and how he would go into school and tell everyone about it, when . . .

'Oh NO!'

It was Mum. She had gone to answer the door before coming in to breakfast. Wilf had heard the doorbell and heard her talking to someone. He went running to see what the problem was.

'LOOK!' Mum wailed.

She was standing next to a huge cardboard box, the contents of which were spilling all over the hallway. In her hands she was holding what looked like a mass of red fluff and a small red ball which looked a bit like a tomato. And her face was a picture of misery.

Grandma came out of the kitchen behind Wilf. 'Oh dear,' she smirked, when she saw the box.

'What's happened, Mum?' Wilf asked.

Meena appeared at the top of the stairs looking sleepy. 'What is it, Mummy?'

Mum sat down heavily on the bottom step. 'My internet order,' she said. 'I ordered some lovely new dresses yesterday, but something went wrong with the screen – you remember, don't you, Meena darling? – and instead, I have got some FANCY-DRESS outfits!' She waved the mass of red fluff and the red ball, and Wilf now saw they were a clown's wig and red nose.

Grandma was biting her bottom lip very hard.

Meena flashed a cute smile. 'You did say you thought they were *fancy dresses*, Mummy,' she said. 'And you said you wanted a *new look*.'

Grandma let out a small strangled noise. 'You've certainly got that,' she said.

145

Mum frowned. 'Did *you* have anything to do with this?' she asked Grandma.

'I wasn't even here!' Grandma protested.

Wilf shot his sister a pointed glance. 'It's probably her fault,' he said.

'Is NOT!' Meena shouted, stamping her foot. 'Mummy, Wilfie is bein' nasty again!'

Grandma was shaking uncontrollably with the giggles now.

'Oh, for goodness sake!' Mum said. 'This is not funny.'

'Clown outfits are pretty funny if you ask me,' Grandma squeaked.

Mum glared at her. 'I'm not keeping it anyway. I shall have to send the box back this morning. Grandma will look after you both while I'm at the post office, won't you, Grandma?' she said firmly.

'Erm, Wilf and I were going to get Titch ready for the show actually,' Grandma replied. 'Could you not take Meena with you?'

'It's all right,' Meena piped up. 'Meena will be very, *very* well behaved.' She dipped her face and fluttered her eyelashes.

'There's a good girl,' said Mum.

Wilf eyed his sister curiously. He was sure he had noticed her cross her fingers behind her back when she had made her promise to Mum.

CHAPTER 17

WHO'S THE SCAREDY-CAT?

Titch was not sure how she felt about being lifted out of Brian's hutch again, but she was determined not to show her nerves to her hysterical housemate.

'Where are they taking you?' Brian cried as he watched her being caught and taken out by Wilf. 'I thought you were going to help us? I thought you were going to be our spy?'

'It seems something more important has come up. Apparently I am going inside to be made ready for a "show",' Titch said. 'I don't know what that is, but maybe this is my chance to get out of this madhouse and go looking for adventure. So long, farewell!' she cried from under Wilf's arm. 'Been nice knowing you!'

As she left the garden, she heard the guinea pig shrieking, 'Don't do anything I wouldn't do!'

'Which leaves what exactly?' Titch muttered. 'If I followed that rodent's advice, I would only get out of bed to eat and use the loo. Whereas *I* am going to do something marvellous – just you wait and see, Brian.'

Wilf had done a lot of research about the show to make sure that he and Grandma did everything properly.

'It says on the website that you need to wash and blow-dry the hens,' he said. 'Do you think Mum will let me do that?'

'Mum's busy taking her order back to the post office, so she won't know,' said Grandma with a wink.

'And what about Meena?' Wilf asked.

'I'll take care of her,' Grandma assured him. 'Let's put Titch in Ned's cat box for now – the one we use to take him to the vet. I'll keep an eye on her and keep her safe while you go and find shampoo and towels and a hairdryer.'

Ned was winding his way in and out of Wilf's legs as Grandma said this. He hissed at the words 'vet', 'shampoo' and 'hairdryer'. Titch immediately set up a dreadful racket.

'I'll put Ned outside too, I think,' said Grandma. 'He's upsetting Titch again.'

Soon Wilf was busy washing and grooming Titch. She was quite flappy at the shampooing stage, but when he began rinsing her in nice warm water she sat happily in the washing-up bowl and did not make a fuss. Once he had the hairdryer on her, she half closed her eyes and started making funny purring noises; it was as if she had gone into a trance.

Grandma put her head round the door to see how Wilf was getting on. 'She is starting to look really lovely!' she said. 'See how her feathers are fluffing up? Her beautiful lavender colour is coming out again. She had got a bit messy after her night on the tiles, hadn't she?'

Wilf beamed. 'Mum will be proud of her too,

won't she, Grandma?' he said.

'Let's hope so, dear,' his grandmother replied.

Ned was very disgruntled at being thrown
unceremoniously out of the house. 'Stupid,
ungrateful hen,' he grumbled as he stalked along the
window ledge of the utility room. He looked in on
Titch, who was having the finishing touches done to
her feathers. 'I don't know why I bothered saving her
from the fox. So much for helping us get our revenge
on the Terror. If she likes all that fuss, perhaps she
would like being dressed up in dolls' clothes as well.
Huh! She thinks she's so clever. As if she's going
to be able to make a break for it at this show she
was twittering about. She doesn't stand a chance.
Everyone knows humans keep birds in cages. They
won't let her out of their sight for a moment.'

He tapped on the window to try to get Titch's
attention, but her eyes were closed in bliss as the
hairdryer warmed and fluffed her plumage.

Ned sighed heavily. 'I'm wasting my time. I should

152

be spying on the girl myself. *I* still have to live here. And *I* am going to get my own back on her whether Titch is here to help or not.'

Ned leaped from the window ledge outside the utility room and landed with a thud on the one looking into the sitting room. There was not really enough space for him on the ledge, so he had to lean his flanks against the glass to stop himself from losing his footing. He was worried that he had made too much noise with his landing, but, luckily for him, nothing was likely to disturb Meena at that moment as she was thoroughly absorbed in watching television. Grandma had felt that this was the only thing that seemed likely to keep her out of mischief.

Ned peered through the window. Meena was sitting on the sofa, her legs tucked under her, while she contentedly munched on a stash of biscuits she had managed to hide in her pockets.

'Maybe I can search through her room to see if there are any clues to what her weaknesses are,' he said to himself. 'She must be frightened of something.'

He found that the sitting-room window was open a crack. He approached the gap cautiously, measuring it with his whiskers.

'Hmm, I should slip through here no problem,' he muttered.

But, embarrassingly, Ned's whiskers had not grown in proportion to the width of his belly, and so he was forced to suck in his tummy to be able to squeeze through.

There was a heart-stopping moment when, at his widest point, it seemed unlikely that he would

manage to get in without alerting Meena to his presence. But then there was a burst of canned laughter from the television and Ned was able to use the noise as cover so that even when the window rattled behind him Meena did not notice.

'Phew! I'm in,' he said as he leaped relatively soundlessly down behind the sofa.

'Aieeeeeek!'

Ned froze at the unearthly, high-pitched noise. 'What was that?' he breathed. He crept very softly along the edge of the sofa and was just about to poke his nose round the side when . . .

'Aiieeeeek!'

Another ear-splitting shriek assailed poor Ned. The cat scuttled back to safety behind the sofa.

The girl is clearly terrified of something, Ned thought. And whatever it is, I'm not sure I want to get involved. It might be . . . wait a minute! He checked himself as something occurred to him. 'This is *exactly* what I was hoping to find out!' he muttered. 'The whole point of my mission was to sneak up on the girl to see if there was anything we could use against her. So all I have to do is take note . . .'

Meena's face was white and her eyes were wide with terror. She had paused, mid biscuit-crunch, and her chocolate-smeared mouth hung open, giving her the appearance of a startled goldfish.

'This is it, Ned my lad,' the cat told himself. 'Observe carefully so that you can report back to base.'

He followed Meena's gaze to the television, where a ghastly face filled the screen. It was white with huge eyes and an even huger mouth outlined in blood-red. Suddenly a dark, caped figure appeared behind the face and said, 'Mwah-ha-ha-haaaaa!'

'Aiiieeeeek!' the face screamed in response.

And, 'Teeheeteeheeheeeeee!' giggled Meena, dropping the half-eaten biscuits and cackling in delight. 'Silly old clown. What a scaredy-cat. Oh, hello, Neddie-Weddie,' she said, catching sight of the cat skulking at her feet. 'Are you being a scaredy-cat

156

too?' She sniggered at her own joke. 'Why don't you come to have snuggles with Meena then?'

Ned swallowed drily. The scene he had just witnessed had confused him and scared him in equal measure so that he was now rooted to the spot. He realized now, too late, that the scream had come from the television, not from Meena.

'Come to Meena,' she crooned, her blue eyes darkening with glee. 'Come and play. You can be the clown and Meena will be the baddie.'

'No-no-no-miaoooooooow!' Ned howled, but he was not quick enough to escape Meena's sticky, chocolatey grasp.

CHAPTER 18

WAR ON THE TERROR

Half an hour later, Ned was a shadow of the intrepid feline he had been earlier that day. Inspired by both the fancy-dress outfit and the television programme, Meena had raided her mother's make-up box.

Ned had been subjected to a full makeover with Mum's lipstick and eyeshadow while Meena attempted to draw a clown's face on him. When this had not worked particularly well (she discovered that fur is not an easy surface on which to apply make-up), Meena had tipped out the contents of Wilf's paintbox, which she had filched from his bedroom, and had used the brightest and most eye-catching colours to paint over Ned's features. The result was a highly colourful cat covered in big polka dots of pink and blue, with eyes and mouth messily outlined in green and red.

'Look, Neddie-Weddie,' Meena said, holding up a mirror. 'What a beautiful pussy you are. Now off you go and leave Meena in peace.'

'Leave *you* in peace?' Ned hissed as he shot out of Wilf's room. 'You have asked for it this time, young lady. I shall never leave you in peace ever again!'

Ned went straight to the kitchen in search of help. He stopped only once to try to lick himself clean, but the taste of the make-up and paint was dreadful.

'How am I going to get this disgusting stuff off me?' he panicked. 'I need Wilf. He is the only one who will be gentle enough. Not that I can bear the thought of being washed . . .'

But the only creature in the kitchen was Ringo, for both Wilf and Grandma were still busy with Titch, and Mum had not yet returned. Ned decided against waking the snoring dog.

'The last thing I need is that dreadful hound leaping at me and licking me all over,' muttered Ned. 'He would be sure to be sick from the effects of swallowing so much paint.'

Ringo was twitching and moaning as he dreamed of catching the squirrel that had got away up a tree. In his dream, Ringo was a superhero. He could levitate up to twenty feet. No squirrel was safe. He sighed a happy sigh and turned over in his basket.

Ned froze when he saw Ringo move, but when he realized the daft dog still had his eyes closed he knew he was safe.

I shall have to take matters into my own paws and have a dip in his water bowl, Ned thought. Desperate times call for desperate measures. And I need to clean up and go back to stalking the girl as soon as possible. This is war!

Ned glanced around to make sure no one was watching, then he took a running leap at the dog's bowl and performed a perfect belly-flop. His aim had been to splash about in the water for as long as he could bear it, and then to roll around on the doormat to dry himself off, as he had seen Ringo do after many a wet and muddy walk.

Unfortunately he had yet again failed to make allowances for his size, and rather than going for a quick dip he had managed to get himself well and truly wedged into the bowl so that now not only was he soaking wet but he was also stuck.

'Miaaaaoooooow!' he groaned. 'Help! Somebody, help!'

'Roooff?' Ringo said sleepily. Then, 'Raaaaaoooooouuu!' he yelped in delight, leaping from his basket and hurling himself at the poor cat.

'Will you get off me, you brainless hound!' Ned shrieked, pedalling his claws wildly at Ringo, who was bouncing excitably at the cat, slobbering over him and trying to pick him up in his jaws. 'This is not a game! It's me, Ned. I'M STUCK AND I NEED YOUR HELP, NOT YOUR TONGUE IN MY FACE!'

'What on earth . . . ?' Grandma had come in to see what the noise was all about. She took Ringo by the scruff of the neck and threw him out into the garden. Then she came back for Ned.

'How did you get in *there*?' she exclaimed. 'You are the limit! I put you outside, and that is where I want you to stay!' And she scooped him up unceremoniously and held him at arm's length. 'You can dry off out there with the dog. Honestly. I thought cats hated water!'

'Miaaaaoow!' said Ned indignantly.

At least, thanks to the water and Ringo's enthusiastic slobbering, he was back to his original colour.

Grandma let out a giggle. 'Actually, the wet look suits you – it's quite slimming!'

Ned hissed crossly, but Grandma had opened the back door again and dropped him on to the patio. He hissed again and stalked off, his tail high in an attempt to preserve his dignity.

'And stay out of the way while we finish with Titch, do you hear?' she said, slamming the door behind her.

'What is you doin', Gran'ma?' Meena lisped.

She had watched the whole scene with considerable delight. Ned had got an awful lot more than even she had bargained for that morning. She let slip a satisfied grin.

Grandma eyed her granddaughter cautiously. 'Meena dear, don't creep up behind people. It's not nice.'

Meena immediately stopped grinning and put on her wide-eyed look. 'Meena didn't creep, Gran'ma. Meena was lookin' for you. What is you doin' with Wilfie anyway? Can Meena play?'

Grandma chewed her lip as she thought of the careful and loving way Wilf was grooming the hen and then considered the state in which she had just found Ned. She scrutinized Meena's face again, but the little girl looked as innocent as a kitten.

'No, dear, it's all right,' she said. 'I don't think Wilf needs any more help. He's nearly finished. I know, why don't you make something with Grandma?' she suggested.

Meena shrugged. 'OK.'

Grandma began rummaging in the cupboards, looking for ingredients to make a cake. 'Ooh, what's this?' she said, picking up some brightly coloured packets. 'This is perfect – nice and easy and quick to make. Meena dear, come and wash your hands while I get some bowls and things out.'

*

Ned was extremely put out by the treatment he had received at the hands of Meena and Grandma.

'I will watch them while they are in the kitchen to see if I can pick up any clues,' he told himself. 'They may let slip some piece of information that could be useful in my War on the Terror.'

He found his way around to the French windows and sat, pretending to wash himself very thoroughly.

He was rewarded by the sound of Meena whining as Grandma began to explain what they were going to do.

'Meena doesn't want to do borin' stuff with Grandma,' she was saying.

'But it won't be boring, darling,' Grandma assured her. 'I've found some lovely things for us to have a play with – look.'

Ned crept closer to the glass to catch a glimpse of what the old lady was showing the girl. He could not make head nor tail of what he saw.

At first glance, the kitchen table appeared to be covered with a jumble of red plastic shapes. But as

Grandma picked each shape up in turn and showed it to Meena she said, 'Look, here's a lovely pussy cat, just like Ned . . .'

It's nothing like me, Ned thought. It's red and hollow and it has horrible, staring, vacant eyes!

'. . . and this is a chicken, like Titch,' Grandma went on, 'and a doggy, like Ringo. Shame they don't make moulds in the shape of guinea pigs, but we have got a bunny one, look.'

'Meena don't like bunnies,' Meena muttered.

'Moulds? In the shape of animals?' Ned said to himself. 'No idea what this is all about, but it is intriguing. I must

166

remain calm, think logically and observe very, very closely,' he murmured.

He hid behind a plant pot and watched.

Grandma was holding one of the strange animals in one hand and a small packet of something in the other. 'I thought we could make a surprise for Mummy and Wilf,' she was saying. 'Let's have some fun with these.' She waved the cat jelly mould at Meena.

Meena shrugged. 'S'pose,' she said.

'We'll use the microwave – you can push the buttons, if you like,' Grandma told her. 'And then we put the moulds in the fridge and wait for a few hours.'

'Few hours?' said Meena. 'BORING! Meena don't wanna wait few HOURS!'

Grandma sighed. She picked up a packet of jelly and handed it to Meena. 'Can you open this for Grandma, please?' she asked.

Meena sulkily snatched the packet from Grandma and ripped the packaging off. And immediately let the contents drop to the floor.

167

She had gone rigid. Her face was drained of all colour and stretched into a mask of horror. She reached up on to the tips of her toes and seemed to grow to twice her normal size.

'URGHHH!' she cried.

Ned was now pressed up to the window, entranced by the performance. 'At last! Something has upset her! I must watch closely,' he muttered.

'URGHHH!' The little girl was yelling and screaming now, throwing her hands in the air. Then she lunged across the table and swiped at the animal jelly moulds, sending them clattering on to the floor. 'Yucky, sticky, wobbly, HORRID!' she shouted. 'It's jelly – JELLY! Grandma knows Meena HATES JELLY!'

Ned's eyes opened wide with interest.

Grandma paled. 'Oh dear, oh dear, I didn't know that!' she said. Then, 'Oh!' She tottered backwards in shock, losing her balance. 'OH!' She knocked into the kitchen table, sending the rest of the moulds skittering across the tiles.

168

The ruckus brought Ringo crashing back into the house through a gap in the door.

'Horrrouu?' he said as he gazed around him.

He took one look at Meena, who was now in full tantrum mode, stomping and screaming, and bounded up to her bravely.

Then, 'Raaaaoooooooo!' he cried, leaping up and barking ferociously like the superhero he had been in his dream.

Typical, thought Ned.

'Waaaaaaah!' said Meena.

'Rrrrroo?' asked Ringo.

He saw that Meena was yelling and pointing at something on the floor at her feet. It was something red and sweet-smelling and sticky. Something delicious.

Ringo pounced, swallowed, chewed – and was immediately sick all over Meena's shoes.

That was when Mum came home.

'OUT, RINGO!' she shouted, opening the French windows. 'GET OUT! NOW! YOU STUPID, STUPID DOG!'

CHAPTER 19

IT'S NO YOLK!

Ned used the confusion to his advantage and slunk in through the open doors as Ringo was booted outside, whimpering, with his tail between his legs.

'Not so clever now, eh?' Ned sniggered as he slipped past.

He hid behind a chair and watched and waited as Meena was comforted by Mum.

She pulled her daughter on to her lap and held her tight while the child worked her way through her tantrum. 'Meena, that's enough,' said Mum. 'Why don't you go and play outside while Mummy clears up this mess?' she suggested.

'MEENA DON'T WANT TO!'

'Meena . . .' said Mum. She twisted her daughter round on her lap and fixed her with a look that had an immediate effect.

The little girl's angry red face immediately calmed. It was as though someone had flicked a switch in her brain, and with one shuddering sob she made herself look small and vulnerable once more.

'Yes, Mummy,' she said in her soft, lisping baby voice. 'Sorry, Mummy.'

And she slid off her mother's lap and tottered out into the garden, hiccuping softly as her sobs subsided.

Ned breathed a sigh of relief that he was safely indoors. He did not hold out much hope for Ringo's safety with Meena in that mood, but told himself he had more important things to think about, as he listened to Mum and Grandma arguing about the mess in the kitchen.

'What did you think you were doing?' Mum was shouting again. 'You know she doesn't like anything sticky! She has hated it ever since that horrible incident at the party when that child stuffed jelly down her neck. She took weeks to recover from it. We had nightmares and tears – it was dreadful! I cannot cope with a replay of that. What were you thinking?'

'I didn't know. Or – well, I must have forgotten,' said poor Grandma. 'I thought I was helping by keeping her out of the way—'

'And where is Wilf?' Mum butted in.

'He's – he's getting ready for the show,' Grandma stammered.

'What show?'

'The chicken show – oh, it doesn't matter. We'll be out of your hair for the rest of the day,' Grandma said. She was beginning to feel cross at being shouted at.

'*Chicken* show?' Mum scoffed. 'Whatever next. See if you can't lose the blooming thing while you are there, can't you?' she snapped as she scooped up the jelly moulds and put them in a bag. 'Chicken shows, fat cats, mad dogs, biting guinea pigs, internet disasters, screaming children. No wonder I need anti-wrinkle gel,' she muttered to herself. 'I'm a nervous wreck. It's no joke looking after you lot.'

173

'And it's no yolk taking care of Titch!' Grandma laughed.

'Oh, stop it!' Mum snapped. She dumped the remaining packets of jelly together with the animal moulds into the bin and banged the lid shut with a flourish. Then she flashed a look of triumph at Grandma and swept out of the room.

Grandma huffed, turned on her heel and left the room as well.

Ned waited to make sure that he was truly alone at last, then he came out from behind the chair.

'Well, I'll be blowed,' he said to himself. 'I've never seen Meena get so upset about anything before. I think there could be something in this. I believe we could use this jelly stuff to teach that girl a lesson.'

He jumped up on the work surface and stalked along, sniffing at utensils and chopping boards and cookery books. Then he noticed one of the colourful packets which had not made it to the bin along with all the others.

He could see it was orange jelly. He glanced quickly at the instructions on the packet. 'Let's see,' he said. '*Chop up into cubes, pour on boiling water* . . . Hmm, that part sounds tricky, but perhaps with some help . . . *Top up with cold water . . . Leave to set.*'

He sat back on his haunches and washed each paw and preened his whiskers as he pondered. 'I think we could do this,' he said to himself. 'I would need a little help from my friends, but yes, yes, I can feel a plan forming.'

And with a sinister smile he leaped down and slunk away to do some proper thinking.

CHAPTER 20

THE POLE TREE SHOW

Wilf was over the moon with the results of his poultry-pampering.

'Look, Grandma!' he cried as his grandmother came into the utility room. She was frowning, but Wilf was too excited to notice. 'Doesn't Titch look beautiful?'

Grandma sighed. 'She does. Come on, let's go. Before any more disasters happen.'

'What disasters?' Wilf asked.

Grandma smiled at her grandson's face, a picture of simplicity and innocence. 'Nothing, dear,' she said. 'I'm sure the next few hours will be blissful.'

They drove to the show in silence. Wilf spent

the time day-dreaming what it would be like to win first prize. Grandma spent the time rerunning the argument with Mum and wishing she had come up with some better one-liners to shut Mum up for a change. Titch spend the journey with her head under her wing, plotting feverishly how she would escape once she was let out of the cat box.

'I will never have to share living quarters with that smelly guinea pig ever again!' she was thinking. 'And I will be able to spread my wings and I may even start laying eggs again once I get some peace and quiet. All I have to do is flap very hard the minute Wilf opens this cage. He will not be able to hold on to me and I will be FREE!'

Unfortunately for Titch, such an opportunity did not present itself. It was not Wilf who got her out of the box. It was not Grandma either. It was a pair of very large, very strong hands, which did not seem to flinch when she tried to scratch and peck them. Her eyes were covered by the fleshy fingers too, so she could not make out her surroundings.

'Feisty little fowl, ain't she?' said a deep voice. 'Luverly plumage though. Bootiful colour.'

The speaker had to shout above the racket around him. It sounded to Titch as though every chicken and cockerel in the world had been put into this place and they were all talking and shouting and complaining and showing off at the tops of their voices. She strained to make out what any of them was saying, but it was impossible to make one voice out from the crowd.

And then she was tipped upside down and realized that her bottom was being inspected!

'Oh, the shame!' she squawked, adding to the pandemonium. 'I am very glad indeed that cat is not here to witness this. Or the guinea pig, for that matter.'

'Very good, very good,' said the deep voice.

Titch felt herself flipped up the right way, but before she could struggle she was put straight into another cage.

'Leave her here for now, young 'un,' said the voice,

which Titch could now see belonged to a very large man in a flat cap. 'We'll take a look at all the others. Prizes in a couple of hours. Why don't you take a look around?'

'Come on, Wilf,' said Grandma. 'Titch will soon settle down.'

'No, I will not!' Titch clucked.

She warbled and flapped, but no one took any notice. She watched as Wilf and Grandma walked away.

'What am I going to do?' she said.

Wilf turned to give her a cheery wave.

'Get me out! Get me out of here!' she cried in a desperate last attempt to get his attention. But he simply grinned, turned away from her and was gone.

'Oh no, oh no, oh no!' clucked Titch.

'Oh, do shut up,' said a voice, strong and proud against the background of the other birds' nervous clucking.

'What? Who? Where?' said poor Titch, turning round and round in fright.

179

'I'm in the cage next door,' said the voice. 'You won't be here for long. Just sit tight until the judging. It's a foregone conclusion anyway. I usually clean up when it comes to the prizegiving.'

Titch tried to look through to the next cage, but that wall was solid. She could only see out of one side of the cage. 'I can't see you. Who are you?'

'You can't see me because they don't trust us not to peck each other through the walls, so they block them off. Of course, some of the poultry here are so common, that is exactly what they would do. Not I. I am a Barbu d'Uccle bantam cockerel. My name is Napoleon and I always win, due to my magnificent, richly coloured plumage. It is a shame you can't see me really. I saw *you* when they

180

put you in your cage and I am sorry to say you've had a wasted journey. I don't think you stand a chance with your rather – er – *grey* little feathers,' he crowed.

Titch clucked irritably. 'It's a good job I'm not interested in winning then,' she said.

'Cock-a-doodle-doooo me a favour!' laughed the cockerel. 'Everyone here is interested in winning. Why else would you be here?'

Titch gave a loud squawk. 'Beeeeruuuuck! If you must know, I am here to do something marvellous. I am going make a break for freedom. I am going free range! I am going to ESCAPE!' she shouted.

At that, the racket in the room stopped abruptly. There was a pause and then a small voice said, 'Escape?'

'Escape?' said another.

'ESCAPE?' chorused some more.

Then, 'HAHAHAHAHAHAAHAAA!' came a volley of sneering laughter.

Napoleon crowed sharply, 'Cock-a-doodle-doooo shut up, you lot!' he shouted.

The noise abated slightly, dropping to a low murmur of gossipy chit-chat, so that Titch could now hear Napoleon saying, 'Why on earth would you want to escape? Where would you go? What would you do?'

And so Titch found herself filling Napoleon in on the recent events in her life.

'So you can imagine my distress when I was thrown in with a guinea pig!' she scoffed, as she finished the story.

'A pig you say?' the cockerel interrupted. 'Well, you could have done worse. Pigs are a wonderful deterrent to foxes, you see—'

'No! Not a pig – a GUINEA pig,' said Titch crossly. 'Oh, never mind. Let's just say that I do not appreciate sharing my home with a fussy busybody. Nor do I appreciate being manhandled by a beastly child who seems to think animals are there to be tortured and frightened just for her pleasure!'

And she went on to describe what had happened to Ned and Brian and how she was terrified she would be next. 'If I had wanted to escape before arriving at that madhouse, I certainly am desperate to escape now! In any case, there is no chance of my doing anything marvellous if I stay there,' she finished.

'I think you are being rather selfish, if you don't mind my saying,' said Napoleon.

'Actually I do mind you saying!' Titch said indignantly. 'I haven't even met you properly. How dare you—'

'Just listen,' said the cockerel. 'You say you want to do "something marvellous"?'

'Yes,' said Titch.

'Has it not occurred to you that you could achieve that simply by going back to the place you call a madhouse?'

Titch paused. 'I – I don't know what you mean,' she said.

'Think about it,' said the cockerel. 'Those other animals clearly need a superior brain to help them out of their predicament. You may not have the

183

looks –' he coughed – 'but you are clearly no birdbrain if you have managed to escape from a chicken run.'

Titch thought carefully for a minute and then said, 'Though it pains me to say it, I think you might be right, Napoleon. I should help my friends.' For, she realized, that is what the other animals could be, if only she let them. 'They have suffered for too long because of that nasty girl. If I really wanted to do something marvellous, I could do it for my friends.'

They were interrupted at that moment by the deep voice of the man in the flat cap who was calling for silence.

'And it is my great pleasure to announce the winner of the bantam class,' he said, above the noise of the gossiping poultry. 'This year's prize goes to the beautiful, characterful Lavender Pekin, shown by Wilfred Peasbody.'

There was a roar of applause from the crowd and a surge of clucking and crowing of disgust from the other cages.

'Well, it looks as though *someone* thinks you have

184

beauty as well as brains,' sniffed Napoleon. From the change in his tone of voice, his feathers had quite clearly been ruffled. 'Good luck to you, is all I can say. Although I can't see what use a little hen like you is going to be against a nasty human child intent on evil. If I were you—'

'Yes, but you're not, are you?' said Titch, puffing out her chest with pride. '*I am me. And I am—!*'

'Titchy!' cried Wilf, running over with a huge pink rosette with '1st Prize' written on it. 'This is for you. Well done, you marvellous hen! I love you,' he said. And he stuck the rosette on the cat box, before gently lifting her back in.

And this time, she did not struggle. In fact, she positively snuggled into Wilf's arms, enjoying the fuss he was making.

'You're the best hen in the world!' Wilf said.

If he could have understood the soft chirruping that came in reply, he would have heard Titch say, 'And *you* are the best boy in the world. I cannot believe that you really are related to that girl. The more I think about it, the more I think that I owe it to *you* as much as to Ned or Brian to teach her a lesson. Yes, this is my chance to do something really marvellous, and no one, not even that girl, is going to get in my way.'

CHAPTER 21

FOX HUNT

Meena had been busy while Wilf was out. She was very, very angry. She was angry with Mum for shoving her out in the garden.

'Like I am a stupid dog, like stupid Ringo,' she muttered, giving the poor pooch a kick as she passed him.

She was also angry with Wilf because he was having a special outing with Grandma.

'And Meena is not allowed to go!' She scowled.

She was angry with Grandma as well for being on Wilf's side about Titch. And she was very angry indeed with Grandma about the jelly.

'Meena HATES jelly,' she went on as she stomped

across the garden. 'Sticky, horrible, slimy stuff, slithering everywhere. Like slugs!'

The world was against her, she decided. And if that was the case then she was against the world.

'Meena is going to do something really, really bad,' she told herself, her eyes glinting. She rubbed her hands together as she thought of what she could do to Brian.

But as she approached his hutch she saw that the door was open.

'Funny . . .' she said. 'Did Wilfie leave it open? Oh, well, stupid Wilfie will lose his ickle lickle guinea pig. Serves him right.'

Then she stopped. There was something sniffing around the hutch. At first she thought it was Brian, roaming free. But then she saw that the creature was bigger than Brian and it had a tail. It was more the size of Ned, although its tail was bushier and had an interesting splash of white at the end of it.

'Oh!' breathed Meena. 'A fox! A *baby* fox.'

She crept round the side of a shrub so that she

could watch it. It was so cute, playing with a pile of autumn leaves, dancing around them and pouncing on them when they moved in the breeze.

'Meena likes the baby fox,' she said to herself. 'Meena wants it.'

She crept up behind it. It didn't hear a thing. It was too busy playing.

Meena took off her jumper and in one quick motion threw it over the unsuspecting fox cub.

There was a muffled yelp, and then silence. Meena

had bundled the cub into a ball in her jumper and was running back to the house with it.

'Meena is going to have some fun now,' she said, laughing as she ran.

Ned had watched the whole thing from up a tree. He had been on his way to tell Brian what he had witnessed in the kitchen, which was why the hutch was open, but had scarpered when he saw Meena making a beeline for the fox cub.

He waited until it was safe, and then jumped down and slipped into Brian's hutch.

'Brian!' he hissed. 'It's OK, she's gone. You can come out.'

'Oh, my rosettes and whiskers! Oh, my claws and paws! Oh, my—' cried the poor guinea pig.

'As I said, she's gone. Oh, for pity's sake, calm down, can't you?' said the cat. 'We'll have no chance of getting our own back on her if you cannot pull yourself together.'

'But you saw what she just did to that fox cub!'

Brian gibbered. 'I mean, not that I care. I can't abide foxes, as you know. But still! I wouldn't wish the Terror on my own worst enemy. And the fox *is* my own worst enemy. Apart from the Terror,' Brian added, getting in a muddle. 'She is my own worst enemy too—'

'Be quiet!' Ned hissed, arching his back.

'Eek!' said Brian, and backed himself into a corner.

'That's better,' said Ned. 'We must not allow ourselves to become sidetracked. The Terror is clearly more of an evil genius than we thought. If she can go as far as kidnapping a fox cub, she must be stronger and cleverer than any human I have ever come across.'

'Either that or mad,' said Brian crossly. He did not take kindly to being told off by the cat.

'Quite,' said Ned. 'How does she think she can get away with it? She can hardly hide the creature in the house.'

'And what will she do when the fox cub's parents come looking for it?' said Brian. 'Which they most assuredly will.'

'Will they, though?' mused Ned. 'I mean, not that I want to hurt your feelings, but can we honestly say that our parents came looking for us when we were taken to live in this hellhole?'

Brian became quite sniffy at this. 'Of course my parents would have come looking for me!' he squealed. 'But they would have found it impossible, seeing as they are in Peru on the other side of the world and, being guinea pigs, they have no means of crossing the ocean of their own accord! I'm sure the foxes will do anything in their power to get their cub back.'

'All this debate is rather by the by if you ask me,' Ned cut in hastily. 'The fact remains that there is now a fox cub hidden somewhere in the house. Have you considered what will happen when the creature grows? He will become as bloodthirsty as his mother and father, and that, my friend, is not good news for you.'

'What about you?' Brian squeaked indignantly.

'I can look after myself,' said Ned.

192

'Oh yes, very good at that, aren't you?' said Brian. 'I mean, you've never been caught by the Terror and dressed in dolls' clothes and pushed in a pram down the stairs only to land on Ringo's head, have you now? Not to mention—'

Ned hissed loudly. 'We are wasting time!' he shouted.

Brian jumped and landed in a heap in the middle of his water bowl.

'You are hopeless,' muttered Ned. 'I can see that if anyone is going to solve this it will have to be me. On my own.'

Ned washed for a moment and then stretched. 'I think we can turn this into a win-win situation,' he said.

'A win-what?' squeaked Brian.

Ned narrowed his eyes. 'Honestly, my intellect is

wasted on you. I have the makings of a plan . . . We need to get the fox off your case, agreed?' he said. The guinea pig nodded. 'He has been hounding you for years, and now that Titch has arrived he thinks the family have laid on a buffet for him.' Ned sniggered at his own joke. 'Ahem . . . I think if we could rescue the cub and restore him to his parents they would owe us a favour.'

'What sort of a favour?' Brian asked, his whiskers twitching anxiously.

Ned flicked his tail. 'A favour that would help us get our revenge on the girl at last,' he said.

CHAPTER 22

HATCHING A PLAN

Titch did not get a chance to crow about her success when she got home. Brian was sleeping and Ned was nowhere to be seen. Wilf had put the pink rosette on the outside of the hutch so that the ribbons were dangling down in front of the wire mesh window.

'At least I will be able to point that out in the morning,' Titch said to herself. Then, as it had been a long day, she nestled down and was soon fast asleep herself.

She quickly found she was having another one of her dreams, a very good one as it happened. One involving a podium and a silver cup and crowds of adoring fans, not to mention an endless supply of crunchy corn and as many juicy earthworms as she could eat.

When she first heard the knocking sound, it seemed as though it was part of her dream: the noise of her own beak tapping against the hard ground for food. But as she blearily opened her eyes and felt sleep drain away from her, she realized that the knocking was very real indeed, whereas the corn and the earthworms were not.

'Oh, for goodness sake, Brian,' she said irritably. 'What are you doing making that racket in the middle of the night? Isn't it enough that you won't leave me alone in the hours of daylight?'

Brian's face, as bleary-eyed and sleep-drenched as Titch's own, appeared from a mound of sawdust. 'What are you doing back here?' he complained. 'I thought I'd got rid of your constant chirping and complaining?'

Titch opened her beak to deliver a particularly disgruntled chirrup when the knocking started up again, only this time it was accompanied by a plaintive wail that even Brian could not accuse Titch of having made herself.

'Holy hay bales!' shrieked the guinea pig. 'That was a . . . I'm sure I recognize that voice . . . It's a . . . a . . .' he stammered.

'Yes, yes!' said the wailing voice. 'It's me. The fox. And I need your heeeellllp!'

'As if,' muttered Titch.

197

'PLEASE!' cried the voice. 'You have to listen to me. There's no time for discussion, no time for argument. Something appalling has happened. YOU HAVE TO HELP ME!'

Titch squawked in disbelief. 'US? Help YOU?' she spat. 'You are joking? I seem to remember that the last time you and I came face to face you were planning on turning me into a gourmet meal. If it hadn't been for Ned, I would no longer be here to help anyone, let alone you—'

'All right! All right!' the fox cut in. 'You have made your point. I am truly sorry that I was so deceitful. I admit that I did have my eye on you as a particularly toothsome snack, but I have seen the error of my ways. I promise I will do you no harm. Please! Come out so that we can talk face to face.'

'I refuse to trust you!' squawked Titch. 'Ned has told me all about you foxes. You woo us with your silky soft ways and make all kinds of promises you have no intention of keeping and then—!'

'Oh, do shut up,' said Brian, for of course he knew

why there was a genuine note of panic in the fox's voice.

'Thank you,' said the fox. 'I will nudge the lock aside with my paw and if you could just push from your side, I think that between us we can get the door open.'

So with much encouragement from Brian, and much chirpy muttering from Titch, the pair of them did as the fox asked. And suddenly there, in the doorway to the hutch, was a long red nose, sniffing its way inquisitively inside.

At the sight of this, Titch definitely felt very flappy indeed. And when a chicken is feeling flappy it makes a lot of noise.

'Beuuuurcck!' Titch cried. 'Ned! Ned! It's the fox! Come quick!'

Afterwards Titch admitted that she had acted without thinking. She said that if she had stopped to consider, she would not have made such a rash move. But adrenalin and fear make a powerful cocktail as poor Brian found when he realized Titch had him round the waist (if a guinea pig can be said to have a waist) and was lifting him off the ground.

'Put me down! Put me DOWN!' he shrieked.

But Titch was a chicken on a mission. She flew in the fox's face, causing him to reel backwards, then she wheeled round, dropped Brian unceremoniously on the lawn and gave the fox one of her kung-fu kicks on the behind. He was already disorientated by

the speed at which things were happening, so it did not take much for him to lose his balance and find himself falling backwards into the hutch.

'Quick, Brian!' yelled Titch.

'I'll help too,' said a voice.

It was Ned. Between them, the three animals managed to push the hutch door shut and slam the bolt home. The fox was now well and truly imprisoned.

The fox stopped sniffing and withdrew his nose. 'Sorry! Sorry!' he cried. 'I did not mean to alarm you. I shall lie low and not intrude upon your living quarters. But if I were you, I would find some other way of making yourselves invisible, for there is a danger greater than any fox out here, let me tell you.'

'What is all this about?' Titch asked crossly. 'You wake us up in the middle of the night, you frighten the socks off us and now you're talking in riddles!'

The fox gave a strange gulping sob. 'He's been

taken!' he said, his voice rising again to the wail that had so scared Brian previously.

'What? Who? Where?' asked Titch.

'It's true,' said Ned, carelessly washing a paw. 'Isn't it, Brian?'

'Yes,' Brian said.

'I don't understand,' Titch twittered.

'My baby. My cub,' cried the fox. 'Taken by a human – a smaller than average human with yellow hair and startling clear blue eyes.' The fox shivered. 'There is something very unsettling about those eyes,' he whispered. 'Who can tell what she has done to our baby?'

Titch looked at Brian. 'The Terror,' she said.

'Exactly,' chorused Brian and Ned.

They explained how Meena treated them and the other animals.

'It's only Ringo who doesn't seem to mind,' said Titch.

'How marvellous it must be to have so little in the way of brains,' sighed the fox.

202

'You – you know Ringo?' Brian asked.

'Of course,' said the fox. 'He comes out into the garden every night, sniffing around at our door, asking if I would like to "come out and play".' The fox tutted. 'As if a working mammal like me has time for that! I asked him about the girl, as it happens, but he really is so clueless, and seems to think the best of everyone. No help to me at all.'

'No,' Titch sighed, thinking of the last time she had seen Ringo, dressed by Meena in one of Mum's blouses, complete with Wilf's school tie and a cycle helmet. The stupid dog had merely run around the garden yapping happily, for all the world as though he was proud to be dressed like a lunatic.

'Whereas we, on the other paw, can be an immense amount of help to you,' said Ned. He stopped to give himself a quick wash, and waited for the fox's reaction.

'You?' said the fox. 'Really?'

Ned looked up sharply. 'We're your best bet,' he said.

The fox nodded sadly. 'I suppose so.'

'So, listen. This is my plan . . .' Ned began.

'It's best we get going right away,' said Ned, once he had outlined the details. 'If we work through the night, everything will be in place for daybreak. Meena quite often wakes up before anyone else *and* she usually comes into the kitchen first to get a snack before going to turn on the television. If we work hard, we can have everything ready for when she walks through the door.'

'But I don't understand,' said the fox. 'Where do I come into all this? And what about my cub?'

Ned sighed. 'Isn't it obvious? If we cause a diversion, you can nip to Meena's room to rescue your cub.'

'Riiight,' said the fox doubtfully. 'It all sounds a bit crazy to me.'

'Well, if you have a better plan—'

'I think it sounds perfect,' said Titch. 'And I for one am more than ready to help you get your own back on that girl. Count me in, Ned.'

After a long battle with the bolt on the hutch to release the fox, the animals made their way as quietly as they could to the kitchen. Titch hopped and flew above the fox and Ned trotted in front. Brian brought up the rear. They had agreed to keep a close eye on the fox; they were not leaving anything to chance where he was concerned.

'I will check the coast is clear,' said Ned. 'Fox, you raid the bin – that's one of your skills, isn't it? But do it QUIETLY for once. Mrs Peasbody put the bin bag out last night and everything we need is in there. Brian, you're going to help me with the jelly-making.'

'I – I don't think I can do that,' Brian stammered. 'I have an aversion to getting my paws sticky, and from what you've said about this jelly stuff . . .'

'Do you want to live in fear for the rest of your life?' snapped the fox.

'It's all I've ever known,' said Brian.

'Exactly,' said Ned. 'And now's our chance to change that.'

205

CHAPTER 23

DON'T COUNT YOUR CHICKENS

The fox crept round the back of the house to where he knew the bin was. Ned was right; he was a frequent visitor to this area, as he found many a tasty morsel that had been thrown away by the Peasbodys, which would feed his family without him having to go to the bother of hunting.

Ned had told him what to look for and, sure enough, after dragging a bin bag out and ripping it carefully with his

teeth, the fox was quick to extract the discarded jelly moulds and unwanted, unopened packets of jelly. He took each mould out of the rubbish and went back and forth through the still unmended cat flap with them, one by one.

'I didn't think you would fit through there,' Ned sneered, as the fox appeared.

'Not all of us have the luxury of being overfed with canned food on demand,' the fox snapped.

Brian stifled a snigger and was rewarded by a clip around the ear from Ned.

'Stop it, you two,' clucked Titch. 'Time is not on our side. We need to get a move on. Brian, come and help me with this.'

She and Brian between them managed to pull and push a measuring jug out of a bottom cupboard.

'Next we need to bite the jelly into cubes,' said Ned. 'Brian, I think you would be perfect for that job. You are always nibbling, after all; those teeth of yours can be put to good use for once.'

'Urgh, no, no!' the guinea pig protested. 'I can't

touch that stuff. It will get stuck in my fur and I shall never get it out of my beautiful rosettes. I can see why the Terror doesn't like it.'

'Oh, shut up!' cried Ned. 'Don't you ever stop whining?' He gnawed off a corner of some orange jelly himself and shoved it crossly into Brian's mouth. 'Maybe that'll stop you,' he muttered.

Brian looked stunned. He paused for a second as if unsure whether to spit out the cube or swallow it down. The decision was made for him when Titch chose that moment to grab him and lift him up on to the work surface to get on with the job in hand.

Brian swallowed. And then something very strange happened.

The little guinea pig's eyes began to bulge out of his head and he gave an enormous quiver as though someone had poured a bucket of iced water over him. Then, just as Ned pushed a pile of jelly packets at him with a muttered instruction to 'get on with it', the guinea pig leaped in the air, tiny paws outstretched in a star formation, and

 208

yelled, 'Aaaaaaaiiiieeee, *caramba*!'

Titch shrieked and flew up on top of a cupboard; the fox whimpered and made a dash for Ringo's basket. Ringo had long ago decided the situation had become far too confusing, and that he was safest keeping well out of the way. He flattened his ears and moved over to let the fox in as Ned hissed angrily.

'For heaven's sake, keep your voice down, you idiot!' Then, 'What in the name of fishcakes is wrong with you?' as the guinea pig began pirouetting across the table top, grinning like a loony.

'I feel goooooood!' Brian sang. 'I feel zany and crazy and full of bubbles! I can do anything! Watch me, watch me!' he cried as he attempted a handstand and fell flat on his face. Then he got up, giggling like a mini hyena, his tiny eyes creased into pinholes, his teeth chattering with glee. He held his furry sides with his tiny paws and laughed until it looked as though he might very well stop breathing.

Ned took a deep breath.
'Holy catnip, he's having a
sugar rush.'

'Don't worry,
Ned!' cried Titch
from on top of the
cupboard. 'I've got
it covered.'

She swooped
down and landed on
Brian, clinging on to
him with her claws
for dear life until he

stopped jumping and dancing around.

'You can't hold me down!' he squeaked. 'I have
seen the light! I have found the real me! Let me at it!
Jelly, jelly! I want jelly!'

Ned let out a fierce miaow. 'Good grief!' he hissed.
'I should have known this plan wouldn't work with
you lot involved.'

'You know what they say!' cried Brian. 'Don't

210

count your chickens! Heheheheeee!'

'SHUT UP!' Ned screeched. 'And you, fox, stop whimpering. Come here. Help me deal with this. We will wake the whole house up if we are not careful.'

And so, while Titch held on to the excitable, squeaking guinea pig, the fox and the cat nibbled the jelly into bite-sized pieces and dropped them into a measuring jug.

'How are we going to boil the water?' Titch asked.

'I have that all sorted,' said Ned. 'We can use this.' He gestured to a large white box with a glass door. 'A microwave!'

Brian wriggled to get one paw free from Titch and agitated it to and fro, grinning wildly all the while.

'What are you doing?'

'A microwave,' he said. 'Heeheeeheee!'

Ned shook his head. 'Imbecile. Why did I ever think you would be of any use to us? Titch,' he said, turning his attention back to the challenge ahead of him. 'Can you leave the stupid creature and help us? I need you to push at the tap until the water is running.'

Titch did as she was asked, leaving Brian to turn round and round in crazy circles on the spot. Ned pushed the jug of jelly towards the running tap and Titch pushed at the neck of the tap until it swivelled round and the water was flowing on to the jelly cubes.

Then Ned shouted, 'Stop!' and Titch flew round and pushed the tap the other way so that the water stopped flowing.

'Now – to the microwave. Fox, I need you again. Your breaking-and-entering skills are required.'

Ned instructed him in how to stand up on the tips of his paws and prise open the microwave door. Then he and Ned nosed the jug of water and jelly across the counter top and into the microwave oven.

Brian, meanwhile, had jumped into a pile of chewed-up bits of jelly and was rolling in it, shouting, 'Look at me! I have found my inner pig!'

'That's it!' hissed Ned. 'If you don't shut up, I'll find my inner tiger. Titch – you'll just have to hold on to him.'

Titch grabbed the sticky, messy guinea pig. There was much flapping on the part of Titch and much squeaking on the part of Brian, but finally she managed to persuade him to come away from the jelly and shut up for the sake of his friends.

'Thank you,' said Ned. 'Let's hope we get

through this without being discovered.'

The melted jelly just needed a top-up of cold water and it was ready to be poured into the moulds.

'This is impossible,' Ned said, frustrated that his plan was taking so long. He sat down and began washing in earnest while he thought what to do.

The fox cleared his throat. 'If I may make a suggestion,' he said.

Ned frowned. 'Yes?'

'Instead of making lots of jelly animals, why don't we make use of the real animals we have?' the fox said.

Ned bristled. 'What? And put our lives in danger? The whole point of this exercise was to avoid the girl laying her hands on us again.'

The fox raised a paw to interject and nodded towards the guinea pig. 'I think Brian may be able to create more of a diversion than a tableful of jelly animals,' he said. 'At least hear me out . . .'

CHAPTER 24

AN EGGS-CITING ENDING

Brian's sugar rush eventually wore off, and he curled up and went to sleep while the others took it in turns to keep watch until the sun peeped over the roofs of the houses. At last, at about six o'clock, Ned heard a shuffling of feet outside the kitchen door, alerting him to Meena's presence.

'Fox! Titch! Everyone!' he hissed. 'Wake up!'

'Whassat?' said the fox, coming out of a deep sleep.

'Eeeek,' whined Brian. 'I've got a headache.'

'Beurrrrck! Shut up, Brian,' said Titch.

'Raoooff?' asked Ringo, looking up hopefully at the bowl of jelly.

Ned shot him a withering look. 'Stay out of this,

hound. Go back to your basket,' he ordered.

'Rooohh,' said Ringo sadly, but he did as he was told.

'Right, so are we clear on what to do?' Ned said to the others.

'Absolutely,' said the fox.

'I'm not sure I want to do this—' Brian began, but Titch had picked him up and plonked him right into the middle of the bowl of jelly on the table.

'Now – hide!' Ned hissed.

Titch crouched down behind the bowl; Ned and the fox hid under the table. The door to the kitchen creaked open, and there was Meena, a nasty smile playing around the edges of her mouth. In her arms was the poor little fox cub, crammed into a pair of doll's dungarees and wearing a pink sock on his head to hide his pointy ears.

Ned realized that the fox's tail was sticking out and tried to grab it to tuck it out of sight, but as he leaned over to do so, lots of things happened at once.

216

'Daddy!' cried the cub, who had spotted the tail and was now struggling for freedom.

'Jelly?' squealed Meena, staring in horror at the bowl on the table.

'¡Arriba, arriba!' yelled Brian, leaping from the bowl, covered from head to toe in orange goo. 'Let me at her! I'll teach her to be cruel. I am invincible! I have Pig Power!'

'ARGHHHHHH!' screamed Meena. 'A jelly monster!'

'Woof-woof-woof-woof!' barked Ringo in delight. He forgot he was supposed to stay in his basket and ran at Meena, jumping and pawing at her, desperate to join in what he thought looked like great fun.

'Beuuuuruck!' shouted Titch, leaping into the air from behind Brian. She picked him up and launched herself at Meena, shoving the jelly-covered Brian into her face.

'ARRRRGHHHH!' The little girl screamed and dropped the wriggling fox cub, whom she had been

trying to hold out of the way of Ringo. The dog was now running round and round her legs so that she was trapped.

'Daddy! Daddy!' cried the cub, scampering over as best he could in his bizarre get-up.

'Thank you, thank you, Ned!' cried the fox, as he licked and nuzzled his little baby. 'Thank you, all of you. You have earned our undying friendship,' he said. 'I promise you will never again be troubled by us foxes.' And so saying, he picked his cub up by the scruff of its neck and raced out through the cat flap at top speed.

Mum was jolted out of a deep sleep by the rumpus and came out on to the landing just as Wilf, too, emerged, rubbing his eyes.

'What's going on?' he mumbled.

'Sounds like someone's downstairs,' Mum whispered, putting her finger to her lips.

Grandma emerged, looking sleepy and dishevelled as well.

'It's probably the dog and cat chasing each other around as usual,' she said. 'Don't worry. Let's go down together.'

The three of them crept on tiptoe down to the hall, where they stopped behind Mum and listened carefully.

'I can't hear anything now, can you?' Wilf said in a rather loud whisper.

'Shhh,' said Grandma. 'What's that funny noise coming from the kitchen?'

They all strained to hear what Grandma was talking about, and sure enough they could just make out a faint whimpering.

'It sounds a bit like an animal in distress,' said Mum, frowning.

'Oh no!' Wilf cried, pushing past both Mum and Grandma. 'I bet she's done something horrible again.'

'Wilfred!' Mum cried, lungeing to grab his arm.

But he was already pushing open the door to the kitchen.

220

'I KNEW it would be you!' Wilf shouted, standing in the doorway and pointing ahead of him.

Mum and Grandma came up behind him. Both of them gasped at the scene before them.

Most of the animals had already gone, but Meena was there, sitting on the floor, her face white with shock while Ringo licked enthusiastically at the jelly on her face. The little girl was staring blankly ahead, whimpering, making the noises the others had heard from upstairs. All around her were opened packets of jelly and the chewed remains of jelly that had not made it into the microwave. There was orange jelly everywhere: on the walls, the ceiling, the surfaces, the cupboard doors – but most of it was all over Meena.

'Meena!' cried Mum. 'What *have* you been up to?'

Meena looked slowly up at her mother and said, 'Meena's sorry, Mummy.'

But the baby voice that usually worked such a charm on Mrs Peasbody did not work this time.

'*Sorry*?' she repeated, her face darkening dangerously. 'SORRY? Is that all you can say? LOOK at this mess! And you told me you didn't *like* jelly! You must have got it out of the bins – oh, my goodness. You are a PEST! I am NEVER letting you out of my sight, ever again!'

Wilf did not understand what had happened, but he had a strong feeling that for once his sister had not caused the mess. He knew how much she hated jelly, so he was pretty certain she would not have got into this mess alone. But he decided to keep quiet and smiled a small smile to himself.

Serves you right, Meena, he thought.

Grandma saw the little smile and put her arm around her grandson. 'Do you know what, Wilf?' she whispered. 'Something tells me your sister has got her *just desserts*.' She chuckled.

Later, back at Brian's hutch, Ned said he did not think Mrs Peasbody needed to have lost her temper like that. 'It's not that I feel sorry for the child,' he said, 'but I think you gave her such a fright, Brian! She wouldn't dare take any of us on again after that performance!'

Brian smiled. 'I wouldn't let her anyway. I have never felt so brave and strong in all my life.'

'All thanks to you, Ned,' said Titch generously. 'I take back all the rude things I said about you when we first met. You are not the Arch-Enemy, after all. And you are most definitely a friend to be trusted.'

'Well, that is kind of you,' Ned purred. 'Although I have to say that it was you who put the most magnificent finishing touches to our little performance. Flying at the Terror with Brian in your claws was pure genius. In fact, I would say that you have achieved your aim of doing something rather marvellous.'

'Thank you,' Titch clucked, bowing her head bashfully.

'So, I have to ask you,' Ned said. 'Are you still intent on escaping? Only I, er, I would rather you

223

didn't. We have all got quite used to having you around the place, you see.'

Titch chirruped with pleasure. 'Oh no, I think I've changed my mind about that,' she said. 'I can see how much I am needed around here. I only have one request . . .'

'What's that?' Ned asked.

Titch looked at Brian. 'If this is to be my home, can I at least be free to eat my breakfast in bed occasionally?'

Brian giggled. 'Sounds good to me,' he said. 'I may well do the same from now on.'

Wilf came out to check on his pets. He needed to be completely sure that they were all safe and sound after the scene he had witnessed in the kitchen.

'Brian?' he called through the hutch door. 'Are you OK?'

The guinea pig came shuffling over, squeaking happily.

'Phew,' said Wilf. 'And Titch – where is she?' he

said, looking around. He could not see the hen. 'Oh no, Titch. Where *are* you?'

But before panic could take hold of him he heard a very excitable noise from Brian's bedding area.

'Beeeuuuurrrck! Berck-berrrck-beuuurrrckkk!'

Wilf laughed. 'You sound happy, Titchy! What's all the fuss about?' He leaned in to get the little hen out for a cuddle – and his hand brushed against something smooth and warm. He took Titch out of the hutch and peered in to get a closer look.

'Oh my! I don't believe it!' he cried. He picked it up in one hand and, holding Titch in the other, he ran back to the house shouting, 'Grandma! Mum! Come and see!'

'What now?' Mum complained as Wilf skidded through the back door, holding out his hand. 'Can't I have my cup of tea in peace?'

'Wilf, are you all right?' Grandma asked.

'I certainly am!' he cried. 'Look!'

And he opened his hand to show them something smooth and creamy-coloured . . .

'An EGG!' they chorused.

'At last,' said Mum, 'one of our animals has done something for us to smile about.'

'Something marvellous, more like!' said Wilf.

'Beuuurrrckkkk!' agreed Titch.

Which, roughly translated, means, 'I thought so too!'

Monkey Business

Anna Wilson

It's so BORING having normal pets!

For Felix and Flo, animals are the NUMBER ONE TOP PRIORITY in life. And although Felix loves his pets (a lazy dog, an angry cat and a noisy hamster), what he really wants is to look after an animal which is EXOTIC and DIFFERENT. Will Flo's brilliant and FOOLPROOF plan get Felix his perfect pet – or will it just send him bananas?

A side-splittingly chaotic story about schemes, dreams and monkeying around.

The Poodle Problem

Anna Wilson

Welcome to the Pooch Parlour,
where mystery-solving has become
this season's hottest new look!

Something very strange is going on in the cosy
town of Crumbly-under-Edge! Join Pooch Parlour
regulars Dash the dachshund and his human
friend Pippa 'chat-till-the-cows-come-home'
Peppercorn as they uncover a dastardly plot
involving oodles of snooty poodles . . .

The first in the bonkers Pooch Parlour series

The Dotty Dalmatian

Anna Wilson

Welcome to the Pooch Parlour,
where pets get pampered
and mysteries get solved!

Mrs Fudge has hired a cool new assistant who
is an instant Favourite with all the dogs. Pippa
Peppercorn isn't so sure – there's something
strange about the new girl. Meanwhile a mysterious
spotty dog is causing havoc around town . . . Will
Pippa and Dash the talking dachshund save the day?

The second in the magical Pooch Parlour series

Chuckle your paws off with

Anna Wilson

Tick the ones you've read!

Get your paws on them all!